Nine Ghosts

by

R. H. Malden

Contents

A COLLECTOR'S COMPANY

The story which follows was told to me rather more than thirty years ago. The narrator was elderly then. He died very soon after the end of the last war with Germany, so there can be no harm in repeating it now. His name, if you want to know, was Arthur Harberton. As he was a young man when it happened to him I suppose it must be dated not long after the year 1870. I made notes of it at the time, and reproduce it now as nearly as I can in his own words.

'Three years after my ordination I was offered a post as a college lecturer at Cambridge. That was the kind of work which I had always thought that I should like, at any rate for a few years, so I accepted the offer very gladly. I have never regretted that I did so; nor that I did not devote the rest of my life to academic work.

'I was not dean of the college, and as in those days the number of Fellows in Holy Order was much larger than it is now it was very seldom necessary for me to be in the Chapel on a Sunday. Accordingly I used to go about the diocese a good deal, visiting the country churches. I don't think that I was under any illusion as to my powers as a preacher, even then. But I thought, without, I hope, undue vanity, that it might be good for village congregations to hear a fresh voice occasionally, and even for the incumbent if he were present. That was not always the case, for I was always willing to take the whole duty of the day if I were asked, so that the incumbent might secure a short holiday.

'As a rule I enjoyed these expeditions thoroughly. They began with a short train journey, followed by a drive from the station, sometimes of as much as ten miles. Country lanes were country lanes then. They had not been blackened with tar macadam and motor-cars were, of course, unknown. An occasional traction engine, preceded by a man on foot carrying a red flag, was the only disagreeable object likely to be encountered. From a dog-cart, which was usually the vehicle which came to meet me, it was possible to see over the hedges and to get a very fair idea of the country as you went along at eight to ten miles an hour.

'My hosts were generally interesting. For the most part they were country-bred men who belonged naturally to their surroundings. Many of them had a wide variety of interests (and sometimes a store of real knowledge) on which they were ready to discourse to a stranger. When I had the house to myself it was amusing to try to deduce what manner of man the owner might be from his books and pictures.

'Most of the churches and a good many of the houses presented features of architectural interest, which appealed to me strongly. Besides, I used to enjoy such conversations as I might have with rural churchwardens, sextons and other parish officials. I remember one churchwarden (a farmer, I think) who had heard that Huntingdon was a fine town. Personally he had never penetrated farther than St. Neots. When I told him that I lived at Cambridge I might as well have said Pekin, or Timbuctoo.

'In another place the village school-master was opposed to elementary education in the abstract: not merely to the particular form of it which he was required to administer. He thought it unsettled children and took them off the land. There was, no doubt, something to be said on behalf of his views; but I couldn't help wondering whether he were *quite* the right man in the right place. Well--no doubt the countryside is more sophisticated now, and I won't bore you with speculations as to whether the gains outweigh the losses or not.

'So, as you see, I had good reason to look forward to these excursions. In fact, I only once got to a place which I should not care to visit again, and that is the one which I am going to tell you about now. All the same, I don't entirely regret that I did go there. Anyhow, it was a unique experience.

'Towards the end of one October term I got a letter from the bishop's chaplain, asking me if I could preach twice on the following Sunday at a village about twenty-five miles from Cambridge--I don't think I will tell you in what direction. The incumbent, it appeared, was not very well, and having no curate was doubtful of his ability to get through the day single-handed. As it would be the second Sunday in Advent it would not be difficult for me to preach at short notice. The collect and epistle for the day provided me with a subject ready-made: a subject, moreover, which I have always found particularly congenial.

'I discovered that there was a convenient train to the nearest station on the Saturday afternoon and from it on the Monday morning, so I telegraphed Yes, and wrote to my prospective host to say when I might be expected.

'It was a little after three when I got out at a wayside station. I was met by a groom with a dog-cart who brought a note from his master apologizing for not having come in person. As I had understood that he wasn't well I hadn't expected him. I will call him Melrose.

'As we drove away from the station I said to the groom, "I hope Mr. Melrose has nothing serious the matter with him?"

'"No," he replied, "but he *du* come over all queer-like at times--so he du. When he have one of his turns--well, it's not for me to be explaining of it, if you take my meaning, Sir."

'I was not at all sure that I did, but thought it would be ill-bred on my part to ask for details. Also I was inclined to suspect that they might be copious rather than enlightening. However, as my companion seemed inclined to talk I did not feel bound to try to suppress him.

'I gathered that Mr. Melrose was wealthy and a bachelor. He had "travelled furren," which was regarded locally as a hazardous proceeding, on the ground that all foreigners are well known to be black, and that they blackamoors might be up to anything. He was much took up with reading: also in my companion's opinion a dubious proceeding. For if there was good in some books there was bad in others, and how'd you know which till arterwards, and then it was done.

'The general impression left on my mind was that while Mr. Melrose might be loved by his parishioners he was certainly feared. I thought that I might look forward to an unusually interesting weekend. As it turned out this expectation was not unduly sanguine, as I think you will agree when you have heard the rest of my story.

'After a drive of about seven miles we arrived. The light was failing, but I could see that the house was an old one. It was rather larger than the average, and I judged that there was probably a considerable garden behind it. I looked forward to examining both more closely between services on Sunday.

'Mr. Melrose made me very welcome. He was a tall man who stooped a little. I set him down as about seventy; probably over rather than under. He had abundant white hair and very prominent white eyebrows. His eyes were dark and his nose aquiline. The general effect was scholarly and striking. He would have been noticeable in any company, and once seen would always be remembered. My first impression was that he was very handsome.'

Here Mr. Harberton paused for a minute or two and then said rather abruptly, 'Did you ever see Thompson (W. H. Thompson, 1866-86.), the Master of Trinity?'

'No,' I said. 'He was some years before my time. But I know the portrait; by Richmond, I think.'

'No, of course you didn't,' he went on. 'Stupid of me. But one forgets how time passes. I don't think the portrait really does him justice. However, if you know it you'll understand what I am going to say.

'I knew him very well by sight and he was one of the most distinguished-looking men I have ever seen. He was handsome if you like, and you couldn't doubt his ability or force of character. You had only to look at him to see that he was a great man. Yet somehow I never could think his face a pleasing one. It always seemed to me to contain great possibilities of evil. I could believe him to be capable of absolutely diabolical conduct.'

'Well,' I said, 'I believe that when Richmond painted Lightfoot he declared that he had never had a sitter whose jaw was so obviously and unmistakably that of a murderer. And I have been told by people who knew the Bishop well that they could believe that he had a naturally violent temper, and that his complete mastery of it was part of his greatness. The same may have been true of Thompson.'

'Yes,' said Mr. Harberton, 'it may. Anyhow, this was the effect which Mr. Melrose produced on me. However, I tried to dismiss it from my mind as foolishness.

'After tea, which we had in a square hall by a log fire, Mr. Melrose asked me to excuse him until dinner-time as he had some letters to write and the post went out at six-thirty. He had a small study on the first floor opening out of his bedroom to which he proposed to betake himself. The library, which was on the ground floor and opened out of the hall, was at my disposal and there were writing materials there if I wanted them.

'The library was a large room, completely lined with bookcases. A cursory inspection of these showed that my host was a man of wide and miscellaneous reading. He seemed to be particularly interested in the later Neoplatonists and to be well supplied with Orphic literature. On a glass-topped table by the window was a collection of Gnostic gems. An Egyptian mummy-case stood upright in a corner. On a table by the fire was a book which he had presumably been reading when I arrived. I picked it up and found that it was Philostratus' *Life* of Apollonius of Tyana. It had been interleaved and was copiously annotated. I should have liked to read some of the notes, but thought that would be impertinent.

'Evidently I was in the house of a scholar whose interests were out of the common run, and the possessor of means which enabled him to indulge them freely.'

'At dinner he proved very good company. He had travelled widely and had visited places which were then very much off the beaten track, such as Sicily and Transylvania. He had spent some considerable time in the latter country and had made a careful study of its grim folklore.

'The dinner was good, and my host exerted himself to be pleasant. Interesting he undoubtedly was, but I was not at all sure how much I liked him. I had a vague feeling that in some way he was playing a part. But I could find no rational ground for my suspicion. And, after all, why should he think it worth while to try to impress anyone so much younger than himself?

'It struck me as curious that a man of his calibre should be content to bury himself in so obscure a place. Of course the country was much more prosperous then than it is now and rural life offered more interests than I fear it does to-day. But this particular neighbourhood was not specially attractive in any way. Most of the land had belonged to the see of Ely and was now administered by the Ecclesiastical Commissioners. I believe that they are always considered to be good landlords, but naturally there are seldom any country-houses other than farms on their estates. I could hardly see my host at ease in the society of farmers, nor could I imagine that they would be able to make much of him. (I had discovered that he did not shoot or hunt, and in those days a man who did neither was very much out of it in the country.)

'When he told me that he had been rector of the parish for more than thirty years I could not help expressing surprise--rather clumsily, I fear, and perhaps not too politely, but I was very young then--and saying something about the solitariness of the life which he led.

'"Yes," he said; "I don't wonder that it strikes you like that. The road from the station is rather desolate. But I have plenty of occupation and interests here; and do you know I find some of my neighbours more companionable than you would expect."

'The last sentence struck me as rather odd, not only in itself but in the way he said it. I felt that there was more behind the remark than I was meant to understand, and did not like the feeling. I liked the laugh which followed it even less. However, there was obviously no more to be said about that. Perhaps he thought I had been rather impertinent, and perhaps he was right.

'After dinner we went into the library for coffee, and somehow our talk drifted to witchcraft, necromancy and kindred topics. I had always taken an interest in such matters, if not a very serious one, and have often wondered what foundation, if any, there is or was for the belief that the powers to which witches lay claim have any real existence.

'At this distance of time I do not mind admitting that as an undergraduate I had once made an essay in Invultuadon. The object was the Vice-Chancellor of the day, whom I did not know by sight. He had annoyed me by refusing to allow a play which I had written to be acted publicly by the A.D.C., on the ground that it was disrespectful to authority. I adopted the only method of retaliation which seemed to be open. I made a waxen image and placed it on my mantelpiece. After some incantations which I thought appropriate (*Flectere si nequeo superos Acheronta movebo* [Aeneid, vii. 12.] is the only line which I remember now) I inserted a pin into one leg. The very next day I heard that the Vice-Chancellor had slipped going downstairs in his lodge and had sprained one of his ankles. I felt that my cause had been vindicated and took no further steps. But, as you will understand, I had not been serious in the matter. I never pretended to think that the accident had been more than a coincidence for which I need not reproach myself. The story leaked out somehow, and one comment on it which came to my ears was "Whole religions have been founded upon less evidence." I will not name the author, but I still think he ought to have known better.

'Mr. Melrose's discourse seemed to me to be a very different story. I could not help thinking that he knew more than he ought about a great deal which was very undesirable. And he spoke with an air of inside knowledge which I found disquieting. His tone was that of a lecturer on a subject which he had really made his own, and he gave the impression of having verified at least some of his knowledge by experiment. I felt that there was something malign about him, as well as creepy.

'Finally, I came to the conclusion that he was like an evil caricature of Dr. Hans Emmanuel Bryerley, the Swedenborgian teacher in *Uncle Silas*. (By Joseph Sheridan Le Fanu.) Altogether I was extremely glad when he suggested a move bedwards, and was at pains to lock the door of my room. Perhaps that would not avail much if it came to the point. But the illusion of security which it produced was comforting.

'I do not know how long I had been asleep when I awoke with the impression which one sometimes has of having been disturbed by a loud and sudden noise. Probably the church clock, I thought, though I had not noticed its strike earlier in the evening. I was just disposing myself for a renewed period of slumber when it struck me that although my fire had burned low the room was curiously light; not with firelight either. I had drawn back the window curtains before going to bed, as I usually did, and the light was coming from the window.

'"Moonlight," you will say. 'But I knew that it was not. In the first place, the moon was several days short of full, and in the second, the light was not coming from a particular point. It was evenly diffused, like daylight on a cloudy day; and no moon could have produced so much light from behind clouds. It seemed to me to have a bluish tinge which was unnatural and unpleasant. I went to the window and looked out. It commanded a view of a good-sized lawn flanked by dark shrubberies of some sort--rhododendrons, I found out subsequently.

'This lawn sloped slightly upwards away from the house, and at the farther end was a low wall with a gateway in it leading to the churchyard. This and the church itself were as plainly visible as if it had been midday instead of just after midnight in December. But everything to right and left was in darkness. I felt as if I were looking down an illuminated tunnel, and it seemed obvious that something would appear at the upper end. I took my courage in both hands and waited. I did not have to wait long. Through the gate in the churchyard wall came my host. He seemed to be wearing a cassock with a long black cloak over it. On his head was a high-pointed cap, something like a mitre, and he carried a short rod in his right hand. He came straight down the lawn towards the house. I wondered whether I was as visible to him as he was to me; and hoped not. Anyhow I felt bound to see the performance through. He was followed by a number of figures: I think about twelve, but I could not be sure.

'Although there seemed to be plenty of light they were somehow curiously indistinct. They may have dodged behind each other from time to time in some odd fashion. Anyhow I found that it was no use to try to count them. They were dressed in long black cloaks with hoods, which prevented their faces from being seen. On the whole I felt glad of that. They moved rather stiffly, like marionettes. Of course their feet made no sound upon the grass. But I was conscious of a faint creaking, the source of which was not easy to determine. It might have been produced by the breeze in the shrubbery; but I did not think that it was.

'The procession advanced until it had reached the middle of the lawn. Then the leader stopped and the others formed a circle round him. Still I could not be sure how many they were. Every time I tried to count them I became confused and arrived at a different result.

'Then they began to dance while he beat time or conducted, however you like to put it, with his wand. They moved more quickly than I should have expected, though they still suggested marionettes. The faint creaking which I had heard before was more audible. There could be no doubt now that it came from the dancing figures.

'Do you remember a story told by one of the minor characters in Stevenson's *Catriona*? About Tod Lapraik, the warlock weaver of Leith. He used to fall into a dwam in his house and once while he was in that state he, or something in his likeness, was seen dancing alone on the Bass Rock "in the black glory of his heart." Those words rose in my mind now. The performance which I was watching seemed to be inspired by an unholy--well, *joie de vivre* I suppose I must call it, though I don't know how far the dancers could be considered to be alive. The whole effect was abominably, indescribably evil. Yet, curiously enough, I did not feel afraid. I have never considered myself a particularly courageous person, and have not had many opportunities of discovering whether I am or not. But anyhow I was not conscious of any fear then. Partly perhaps I was too deeply interested in what I was watching to think of anything else. Also, youth and a good digestion will carry their possessor securely through many of the changes and chances of this mortal life.

'The dance grew faster, and the ring of dancers contracted. As it did so the mysterious light contracted too. I could no longer see the church, or the greater part of the lawn. Only the tall stationary figure with his black-shrouded companions whirling--it had come to that now--whirling round him. The group was illuminated as a particular figure sometimes is upon the stage (spotlight, I think they call it), but as before the light did not seem to be coming from any particular direction. Perhaps this was why I could see no shadow upon the grass.

'In another minute the dancers seemed to have closed in and then (as was perhaps to be expected) the light went out. I could neither see nor hear anything. The garden seemed to be as dark and deserted as you might expect between midnight and 1 a.m. on a moonless night in December. As I turned away from the window I heard the discordant cry of a night-jar (at least that was what I thought it sounded like) very loud and apparently very close to my window. Immediately afterwards I heard a low chuckle. It was not a pleasant one. I felt pretty sure that whatever the joke might be I should prefer not to meet the author of it. I made certain that my door was locked, made up my fire to last until daylight, got into bed and rather to my surprise fell asleep almost immediately.

'It was getting light when I woke. I got out of bed and unlocked my door. As I waited to be called I naturally thought of my experience of a few hours earlier. The more I considered it the less confident did I become that I had not dreamed the whole thing. I have always been an active and vivid dreamer, but have never had a vision of my head upon my bed worth taking seriously; even by the most nasty-minded psycho-analyst who ever came out of Vienna or anywhere else.

'At eight o'clock the butler brought me tea and hot water. On the tray was a note from Mr. Melrose saying that he regretted that he was unable to leave his room. The clerk would show me where everything was in the church. Would I make myself at home in the house and ask for anything I wanted, etc. etc.'

'"Is your master seriously ill?" I asked the man. "Ought a doctor to be sent for, or can you look after him?"

'"No, Sir, not serious. But he don't come down as a rule, after one of his nights, not for a day or two."

'For a moment I thought he was going to say more, but he turned away and began laying out my clothes. So I said something to the effect that old people often slept badly and that no doubt a wakeful night was very exhausting.

'To this he merely replied, "Yes, Sir," and left the room.

'While I was drinking my tea I thought I would look at the lessons for the day, as I should probably have to read them myself. There was a Bible beside my bed and I opened it at *Isaiah* (the first lesson was Chapter 5, as you probably remember), and it so happened that the first words which caught my eye were from Chapter 8, verse 19

Seek unto them that have familiar spirits and unto the wizards that peep and that mutter.

'No doubt a coincidence. But as I dressed I became more and more inclined to think that I had not been dreaming.

'The day passed uneventfully. Evensong was at three, as was not unusual in the country then during the winter months; I must confess that I was glad of this as I did not relish the prospect of coming down the lawn from the church in the dark. Of course it was getting dark by the time service was over, and as I went through the gate leading from the churchyard I had an uncomfortable feeling that my movements were being watched by some person or persons whom I could not see--and not with any amiable solicitude for my welfare.

'However, nothing untoward happened then or during the evening. I went to bed early and slept soundly all night. Next morning the butler brought another note from my host, expressing his regret that he would be unable to see me before I left, the disappointment which he felt at having had so little of my society, and a hope that I had been made comfortable.

'I replied to the first two heads of this communication as politely as was consistent with the truth. As regards the third I could reassure him honestly. I left the house soon after breakfast. The butler had not seemed disposed to be communicative, nor was the groom who drove me to the station. Three days later I went down for the Christmas vacation.'

'Mr. Harberton was silent for a minute or two, so I asked--I must admit with a feeling of disappointment--'Is that all?'

'Not quite,' he replied. 'But for the conclusion of the story you had better read this.'

He handed me a cutting from a newspaper, probably a local weekly, which he took from a large old-fashioned pocket-book. I had seen the book before, as it was his practice to carry it with him. The cutting was from the bottom of a column, so no date was visible. I judged it to be about thirty years old. It ran as follows:

'RECTOR'S STRANGE DEATH

'A painful sensation was produced at [the name of the place was carefully erased] on Christmas morning.

'As soon as it was light the sexton (Mr. Jonas Day) had gone to the church to make up the fire in the stove. As he approached the south door he was horrified to observe the body of the rector lying face downwards on a flight of four steps leading from the churchyard to the rectory garden. He went at once to the house and summoned the butler (Mr. Thomas Blogg) and the groom (Mr. Henry Meekin). They carried the rev. gentleman to his room, but it was all too evident that the vital spark had ceased to pulsate. Dr. Horridge was sent for and arrived a little before ten o'clock. He reported that the neck of the deceased was broken and that death must have intervened some hours before.

'It may be presumed that the unfortunate gentleman had gone to the church at a late hour to satisfy himself that everything was in order for the morrow. The steps were slippery with frost and he did not appear to have taken a lantern.

'The Rev. [name erased] had held the rectory for thirty-two years and the sad occurrence cast a deep aroma of gloom over the festivities naturally incidental to the day.

'The inquest was held at the Fox and Grapes on the 30th ult., Dr. Horridge presiding as Coroner. Mr. Blogg deposed that his master not infrequently went to the church late at night. When asked by one of the Jury if he knew for what purpose, he replied that he had never demeaned himself to curiosity in his master's business. He was warmly commended by the Coroner for his reply.

'Mr. Day deposed that when he approached the body he saw some curious marks on the back of the coat. When pressed to describe them he said "Like muddy claws." Neither Mr. Blogg nor Mr. Meekin had noticed these. The coat was sent for, but it had been brushed. The Coroner thought that they might easily have been made by an owl or some other bird of the night perching upon the body after life was extinct, and by his direction the Jury returned a verdict of *Death by Misadventure*.

'The funereal obsequies were celebrated on the and instant.'

'May I take a copy of this?' I asked.

'Yes, if you like,' said Mr. Harberton. And I did.

THE DINING-ROOM FIREPLACE

Anyone who knows the neighbourhood of Dublin will remember the good-sized country-houses in which it abounds. Most of them date from the eighteenth century, when Irish landowners were prosperous and labour was cheap. Some of them incorporate bits of older buildings which may have begun life as castles of the Pale. Most of them are now in a state of dilapidation which is not unpicturesque, though it would be out of place in England.

Perhaps I ought to have used the past tense. I do not know how many of them have survived the establishment of Eire--or whatever that part of Ireland chooses to call itself nowadays--and I do not feel tempted to go and see.

I am writing of things as they were during the closing years of the reign of Queen Victoria.

It was during a visit to one of them in the autumn of the year 1899 that the experience, I can hardly dignify it by the name of adventure, which I am about to relate befell me.

It belonged to a family named Moore who had inhabited it for several generations. The present owner was a young man, unmarried and in the army. Naturally he could not spend much of his time there and was glad to let it when he could. It had been taken for one summer by some cousins of mine who lived in Dublin, and it was on their invitation that I was there.

I need not try your patience by attempting to describe it in detail. There was nothing very noteworthy about it except an almost ruinous tower at the north-west angle. This was obviously much older than the rest of the house, and we young people thought it ought to contain a ghost. We could not, however, hear of any story to that effect. We explored it pretty thoroughly, but found nothing more exciting than a very large quantity of dust and a few bats. We went there once late on a moonlight evening, but even then could not pretend that we saw or heard anything unusual.

The south side of the house consisted of three large rooms: a drawing-room at the western end, then a dining-room opening out of it and lastly a billiard-room which was also used as a gun-room. Probably, in fact, it had been built as a gun-room and the billiard-table had been added afterwards. It had a door leading into the garden, but there was no access to it from the house except from the dining-room.

The dining-room was hung with portraits of bygone Moores, who had no doubt played their several parts adequately in their generation. But none of them had reached fame and the pictures were of no outstanding artistic merit. The collection as a whole looked well enough, but was not likely to be of much interest, except to members of the family.

One picture there was, however, which did arouse our curiosity. It represented a man of about thirty. There was no name or date upon the frame, but the dress was that of the closing years of the eighteenth century. The most remarkable thing about it was the attitude which the sitter had chosen to adopt. He was astride of a chair with his arms folded and resting on the top rail. His back was towards the spectator, so that his features would have been invisible if he had not been looking over his left shoulder. His face, so far as it could be seen, did not resemble a Moore. The upper part suggested considerable intellectual power; the lower part was not pleasant. The whole effect was formidable and bespoke a man who would be a very dangerous enemy.

The execution was not particularly good; in fact the technique suggested an amateur. But it was impossible not to feel that the artist had caught the likeness of his original well; and difficult not to regret that he had done so. We wondered why such a curious picture, which did not look like a family portrait, should be displayed so conspicuously. It looked as if there must be a story of some sort about it.

A few days later Captain Moore called. He was stationed at the Curragh, and having some business to transact in Dublin very civilly looked in to ask after his tenants' comfort. We ventured to put a question about the curious portrait.

'Yes,' he said, 'it's a fantastic thing, isn't it? Clever in a way though, and I should think a good likeness. But I don't know who it is any more than you do. It isn't one of the family--you'd guess that, I hope, by looking at it. All I know about it is that my great-grandfather--the old boy over there (here he pointed to a portrait of the same period which hung exactly opposite on the other side of the room)--stuck it up about the time of the Union. I rather think he painted it himself. Anyhow he was so keen about it that he left directions in his will that it was never to be moved. So there it's been ever since. I expect there is a story, if I knew what it was. I believe my great-grandfather had been pretty wild in his young days. A lot of his generation were dazzled by the French Revolution, y'know. I dare say it looked better at a distance than at close quarters. But while he was still pretty young--about the turn of the century, I think--he turned over a new leaf, Model Country Gentleman, Magistrate, Churchwarden, all that sort of thing, y'know, and I believe a really good man into the bargain. Very charitable and so on. Not very hospitable though, by all accounts. In fact during the last years of his life when he was a widower he would hardly see anybody, and I believe was nicknamed The Hermit. I remember once when I was a little chap, about six, I think, I was playing in the dining-room on a winter afternoon. I think the nursery chimney was being swept; anyhow I had been sent downstairs for some reason. It was getting dark--and something gave me a terrible fright. The funny thing was that I couldn't say what it was and I don't know now. But I think it was something to do with that picture. I ran screaming into the drawing-room where my mother was and though I couldn't tell her what was the matter, I am sure that she thought it was that. When I had been comforted my father came in (he had been out shooting, I think) and she began to talk to him very earnestly. I wasn't meant to hear and don't suppose I should have understood much if I had, but I do recollect that she said something to the effect that it couldn't go on and that it wasn't as if this were the first time. And he said that he couldn't do--whatever it was she wanted him to do. I suppose now she was asking him to have the picture moved, or perhaps to get rid of it outright and he was reminding her of the clause in his grandfather's will. Of course ninety-nine women out of a hundred would see no reason why the wishes of someone who had been dead for more than fifty years should be allowed to interfere with their own. Anyhow, that was the nearest approach to a quarrel which my father and mother ever had, that I can remember. And the picture stopped in its place, as you see.

'I once asked him about it. He looked very grave and was silent for a minute or two, as if he were making up his mind about something. Then he said, "I'll tell you what I know about it some day, but not just now. You must wait until you are older," and I had to be content with that.

'Both he and my mother died soon afterwards, and I went to live with an uncle on her side (my father had been an only son), and the house was shut up for several years. So I never heard the story, whatever it may be. I expect old Barton at the lodge knows something about it. He's been on the place all his life, and his father and grandfather before him. But I'm pretty sure he wouldn't tell anybody if he did know.'

After Captain Moore had gone I went and examined the picture more closely than I had ever done before. I came to the conclusion that it was a cleverer thing, and a more repulsive subject, than I had thought at first. One thing perplexed me very much. I tried to put myself into the position of the sitter and found that I could not twist my head round as far as his. His chin was almost on his left shoulder. Why had he chosen to be painted in such an unnatural and indeed, as it seemed, impossible attitude? And how had he contrived to sit for it?

I don't think the expression Rubber-neck (which I believe to be American for Sightseer) had been coined then. Or if it had it hadn't crossed the Atlantic. But I can think of no one to whom it would be more appropriate.

A day or two afterwards I happened to see Barton in his garden and thought I would try whether there was anything to be got out of him. Like all his kind his conversational powers were remarkable and he was never unwilling to exercise them. Eventually, I got him on to the pictures in the house, and I thought that he seemed to feel that he was being drawn towards thin ice. How would the like of him know anything about them, or photygrafts either? Sure, I must ask the young master about them, and wasn't he in the house only last week?

I recognized that Captain Moore's estimate of him as a source of information on this point had been accurate. A few nights afterwards when we were all in the drawing-room after dinner I had occasion to go to the billiard-room to fetch a book which I had left there. Dinner had been cleared away, so I took a candle to light me through the deserted dining-room. Just as I was passing the fireplace I was conscious of so strong a draught that my candle guttered and was nearly blown out. I supposed it was a down-draught, due to the large size of the chimney and to the fact that there was no fire in the grate, and rather wondered that we had never noticed it before. It was not a windy night, so that if there were a strong draught now one would suppose that it was a permanent feature of the room, and that whoever sat on that side of the table would want a screen behind his chair. But hitherto no one had made any complaint.

On my way back I was surprised to find the draught equally strong in the opposite direction. It was now sucking inwards towards the fireplace. I held my candle high, shielding it with the other hand, and looked round to see if there were an open window. But the windows were all securely shuttered, and the doors at each end of the room were shut. I could not account for any draught, much less for one which apparently changed its direction, almost as if it were due to the slow breathing of some gigantic creature crouching in the fireplace. While I stood there the inward draught suddenly ceased. After a moment's stillness there came an outward puff--really strong enough to be called a gust--which blew my candle out. This was too much. I groped my way to the end of the room as quickly as I could without stopping to light a match. Once out of the room I felt rather ashamed of myself for having been so easily scared. I suppose that was why I did not feel inclined to say anything about what had happened. Probably I said to myself there was really more wind outside than I had imagined, and of course a rambling old house was likely to be full of unaccountable draughts. Most likely this one depended upon the wind being exactly in one quarter, which was why we had not noticed it before, and more to the same effect, But I did not find this cogent reasoning convincing.

When I went to bed I looked out and everything seemed to be perfectly still. This, I was bound to admit, was as I had expected. Three nights later I had a curious dream. I dreamed that I was in the dining-room, and that the figure over the mantelpiece had come down from his frame. He was seated astride of a chair as he was painted, almost in the fireplace. His back was turned to the room, but instead of having his head upon his shoulder, it was turned away so that nothing could be seen of his features. He appeared to be speaking with great earnestness to an invisible personage who must have been stationed a few feet up the chimney. I could not catch what he was saying, for he spoke very rapidly. But his tones were those of a person in deep distress.

When he had finished speaking there came a rumbling, moaning noise in the chimney, such as is made by the wind on stormy nights. This presently began to shape itself into words. At first they were not at all distinct, but gradually they became clearer, though they seemed to be in a language unknown to me. I wondered whether it could be Irish. The voice spoke very deliberately with a cold malignity of tone which made me feel very thankful that I could not follow what it was saying. There was something indescribably evil about it. It was the most unpleasant sound to which I have ever listened, asleep or awake. If fear can make the hair stand on end I must have resembled a clothes-brush.

At this point I woke, and it was more in obedience to some automatic instinct than to any reasoned courage that I decided to visit the dining-room. I do not know what, if anything, I expected to see. As I opened the door there was a grating sound, as if a chair were being hastily dragged across the uncarpeted part of the floor. But I told myself that that was caused by rats. The house abounded in them and everyone knows that they can make extraordinary noises. I suspect that they are at the bottom of a great many ghost stories.

I advanced to the fireplace, but beyond the fact that the hearth-rug was curiously bundled up into a heap--a circumstance which did not for some reason strike me at the moment, though I wondered about it afterwards--there was nothing in the least unusual to be seen. My candle burned quite steadily as I held it high and looked round the silent empty room. I stared up at the odd, forbidding picture above the mantelpiece, but there did not seem to be anything to be got out of him. Upon the whole I was glad of that, for he did not look like the sort of person I should have chosen for a midnight *tête-à-tête*.

'Well,' I said aloud, addressing the portrait, 'I wish I knew rather more about you. But as you aren't in a position to explain yourself, I shall go back to bed.'

I did so; and slept soundly for the rest of the night.

Next morning I did not mention my dream to anyone else. Perhaps I was a little ashamed of it. Also the walls of Irish houses have even acuter ears than those elsewhere and I did not wish to be responsible for an outbreak of hysteria among the servants.

It so happened that I had no occasion to be in the dining-room alone after dark during the next day or two. Perhaps I was at pains not to be. No one commented upon the curious draught which I had noticed. Indeed I do not think it was perceptible in the daytime. My dreams, when I had any, were, as usual, entirely commonplace.

One evening, when my visit was nearly at an end, one of my cousins and I were sitting talking in the billiard-room after the rest of the family had gone to bed. Our conversation turned on ghosts and apparitions of various kinds; a subject in which we both took a keen if sceptical interest. Dreams and their value (this was before the days of psychoanalysis) and the possibility of their coming true were also discussed and it was past midnight when we got up to go to bed. We then found that there were no bedroom candles for us. Presumably they had been left in the dining-room or in the hall beyond it. The oil lamp by which we were sitting was too big and heavy to take with us. As it was past the middle of September and the day had been wet we had had fires in the sitting-rooms. The dining-room fire had been burning brightly when we finished dinner, so that it was probable that there would still be enough of it left to prevent our passage through the room from offering any insurmountable obstacles. So we put the lamp out and prepared to go.

As soon as we opened the door we saw that our surmise had been correct. There was a sufficient glow in the fireplace to light us down the room. But we had hardly taken a step before we were startled by a rapid thudding sound, such as might be produced by a big dog beating his tail upon the floor. There was a dog about the place, but at night he had his own quarters in the stable-yard. Even if he had not been put to bed then properly--as might very well be the case in a household of Irish servants--he had certainly not been in the dining-room during dinner and could hardly have got there since.

The thudding ceased as suddenly as it had begun. But next moment we were even more startled by seeing the fire beginning to disappear. I remembered a story which I had once read--by H. G. Wells, I think. In it the lights in a haunted room go out one by one and as the occupant rushes to the fire to rekindle them that too dies away into absolute blackness.

But we soon saw that our fire was not going out like that. It was being obscured by some large dark object which was rising from the ground between ourselves and it. It was as if the hearthrug were slowly humping itself into the form of an animal of some kind. It rose and rose without a sound. Soon it was larger than any dog and its movement had somehow an uncanny suggestion of deliberate and malign purpose. Its bulk and outline, so far as we could make them out, suggested a bear more than anything else. But the head was not shaped like that of a bear. There was something more than half-human about the outline which made it peculiarly horrible. There seemed to be a nose not in the least like the snout of any animal. Presently no vestige of the fire was to be seen. Then it suddenly reappeared. The creature, whatever it was, had gone up the chimney.

We felt that the longer we waited there the less we should like it, so as soon as the coast was clear we ran down the room as hard as we could go, keeping as close as possible to the side away from the fireplace.

There was plenty of firelight in the drawing-room and we soon laid hands on our candles and made our way upstairs. Our bedrooms opened into each other and we left the door standing wide. I do not think either of us slept well, but there was nothing to disturb us except the owls, who (we both thought) were noisier than usual.

Next day we told our story to the rest of the family and I added what I had to say about the mysterious draught and my dream. Of course there was only one thing to be done. The whole thing must be laid before Captain Moore as soon as possible.

Meanwhile the doors of the dining-room must be kept locked and meals served in another room, which a house-agent would probably have called The Breakfast Parlour. I was obliged to return to England on the following day, so it was some weeks before I heard the sequel.

In response to an urgent if guarded letter Captain Moore came over from the Curragh as soon as he could get a few days' leave. He soon knew all that there was to tell. His first step was to pay a visit to the lodge, but unfortunately the day before his arrival Barton had had a stroke from which he never recovered. He seemed to recognize his master and to be glad to see him. But he was in no state to be questioned. He died that night. Next day his daughter, who lived with him, told us that after Captain Moore's visit her father seemed to have something on his mind. Just after midnight he sat up and made an effort to say something. The only words she could make out sounded like 'trouble' and 'back of the picture.' Immediately afterwards he fell back on his pillow and expired.

This was something to go upon. The queer portrait must be meant. A step-ladder was procured and Captain Moore and my cousins set to work. It took them longer than they had expected, as the picture was not hung in the usual way. A number of long screws had been driven through the frame, which was very solid, into the panelling of the wall behind. At last they were all got out; not without difficulty, though they did not seem to be particularly rusty. The immediate result was disappointing. There was nothing to be seen either on the back of the picture or the surface of the wall.

Then somebody noticed what looked like a fine crack running across the top of one panel just below the raised frame containing it. Closer examination showed that the wood had been cut through on all four sides with a very sharp knife. A little picking at the top and out it came, disclosing a cavity, obviously the work of an amateur mason, in the thickness of the wall. In it reposed a small book, about nine inches long by five broad. At the top of the title-page were the two words

THE CLUB

and underneath was a list of twelve names; presumably those of the members. Several of them belonged to families still represented in the neighbourhood. The last was Robert Moore, Captain Moore's great-grandfather.

By this time lunch was ready, so further research was postponed.

When the party returned reinvigorated to their task they discovered, as was not unexpected, that what they had found was an informal minute-book.

It was apparently the custom of the Club to dine once each month with one of the members and discuss topics of general interest. The first dinner was held on 14 July 1778. There were notes as to the amount of wine consumed, which need not be recorded here. One would imagine that the members of the Club must have acted on the principle which was adopted subsequently by Mr. Jorrocks--'Where I dines I sleeps and where I sleeps I breakfasts.'

There were also notes of the discussions. These were more interesting. At first they were principally political. The recent revolt of the American colonies appeared more than once, and though no formal vote was ever taken, it was obvious that opinion was divided as to the character of George Washington. Some members regarded him as a high-minded patriot; others as a sordid tobacco-planter who did not want to make any contribution to the cost of the campaigns to which he and his like owed their security and prosperity.

The revolution in France also aroused much interest. General opinion seemed to have been more favourable to it than most people--at any rate in England--would have approved. But the members of the Club were probably all young enough to feel it their duty as well as their pleasure to ventilate opinions which would have shocked their elders could they have heard them.

As time went on the tone of the meetings became less innocent. A certain amount of profanity began to appear, and once or twice some rather vague entries suggested some dabbling in black magic. At one dinner, held in the year 1797, there was a note--'The President's Health was drunk in bumpers with [probably acclamation,' but the fact that the writer had changed his mind more than once as to the proper spelling of the word, added to two considerable blots, had made it indecipherable]. On the next page was a plan of the table with the name of each member against his place. There were six on each side; no one at top or bottom. The top was, however, marked with a X. From this time onwards there were frequent references to The President, but curiously his name was never given. The minutes were usually initialled J.B. James Butler was the first name in the original list, so was presumably that of the senior member. It was not, however, clear whether he was to be identified with the President. Near the end of the book was an entry in a different hand. It ran:

'The Club is dissolved. Lord have mercy upon us.'

It was signed Robt. Moore and dated 23 September, 1799. My odd experiences had culminated on 23 September, 1899. There was nothing else in the cavity in the wall except two small scraps of paper. They had obviously been part of a larger sheet which had been torn up. What had become of the rest it was impossible to say. On one appeared the words *like a bear*, on the other *clean broak*. That was all.

Despite his ancestor's wishes Captain Moore felt justified in destroying the portrait. It was soon hacked to pieces and the bonfire which it made in the garden consumed the minute-book of the Club as well. The panel was replaced and another picture hung over it. As far as I know there were no further disturbances. Perhaps a century is a kind of statute of limitations in such matters. We do not understand them sufficiently to be able to speak positively about them.

It seems pretty clear that at its last meeting the Club somehow got more than it had bargained for. But it is impossible to reconstruct exactly what had happened. Who was the President, and was the last meeting the first at which he was actually present? Was the queer portrait, which was presumably Robert Moore's work, intended to operate as a warning, like the public executions which were then in vogue?

Some years afterwards I happened to find myself sitting next to an Irish clergyman at a public dinner. He was incumbent of a parish near Dublin, he told me. As the evening wore on, and the tide of speech-making flowed strongly, our talk, in the intervals, turned on superstitions.

'It's queer,' he said, 'the way they lay hold of people for no reason that anyone can see. Now there is one grave in my churchyard that the people won't go near. And when we turn in sheep to keep the grass down the farmer always sends a boy to see that they don't graze by it. It's a nuisance, because we always have to scythe that bit--and the sexton doesn't like doing it either. It's an ugly, pompous thing to a member of a family that used to be well known there, I believe, though there's not been any of them about these fifty years. But why there should be anything unlucky or wrong about it I don't know. I'm not sure that the people do. Anyhow, if they do you won't get it out of them.'

'I wonder,' I said, 'whether the occupant is named James Butler and whether he died on 23 September, 1799?'

'Why, yes,' he said. 'But how in the world do you know anything about it?'

'Oh, I used to have relations with whom I sometimes stayed in that neighbourhood.'

I thought that was as much as I need tell him.

STIVINGHOE BANK

The coast-line of Norfolk is one of those which have altered considerably in historic times. Along some stretches the sea has encroached. At low water traces of lost villages can still be seen, and in stormy weather pieces of wood from drowned forests are sometimes washed ashore. At Cromer a lighthouse which I remember has disappeared long since, though it was not very near the edge of the cliff when I knew it. A new one has been built at some distance inland.

Along other stretches the sea has receded and towns which were once thriving ports are separated from it by a wide expanse of marsh, where cattle graze and abundant mushrooms can be found in early autumn. These marshes are intersected by deep and muddy channels up which the tide creeps sluggishly. But even at high water nothing larger than an open boat can use them. The harbours whence the cloth was shipped in the great days of East Anglia, when Norwich was the third city in the kingdom and nearly wrested the second place from Bristol, are almost useless now. The towns which lived by them have dwindled to small villages. Here and there a fine old house may still be seen on the water-front. But for the most part the large and magnificent churches are all that remain of their former glories.

Melancholy as these villages are they have a beauty and dignity of their own. The wide horizon of marsh, beach and sea beyond gives a sense of spaciousness which can hardly be found elsewhere. Anyone who knows them will understand why a Norfolk nurserymaid when taken to Grasmere complained that she felt unable to breathe and that the mountains spoilt the view.

They have always been well known to sportsmen as the marshes teem with wild-fowl in winter.

Of late years artists have begun to discover them. But I must admit that I hope they will never become popular resorts.

It was at one of them, which I will call Stivinghoe, that the experience (it hardly deserves to be called an adventure) which is set down here, befell me some years ago. If, when you have heard the story, you think it rather pointless, that is not my fault. I do not think that I should have admired Mr. Chadband (See Bleak House.) had I met him. But his insistence on what he called *The Terewth* always seemed to me worthy of imitation. And I could not make the story more exciting without departing from the standard set by that eloquent divine.

Stivinghoe differs from its neighbours in the possession of a bank; that is to say a causeway some eight feet high running across the marsh land and projecting beyond it into the sea. I suppose it is natural, as it is not easy to see why anyone should have taken the trouble to construct it. There is a rough track along the top. At the shoreward end the sides are clothed with coarse grass where sea-pinks and yellow horned poppies grow. The last half-mile is sand and shingle. At high water the sea comes up to it on both sides. When the tide is out it is flanked by a wide expanse of wet sand. At the far end there is a little hillock on which are the remains of a ruined chapel. It is as lonely and desolate a spot as can well be imagined. I suppose the chapel had escaped demolition because it had never been worth anyone's while to pull the walls down and cart the material away. It was a cell of the great house of Walsingham and had been established as a place where prayer might be offered continually for fishermen along the coast and all who got their living from the sea.

After the dissolution of the monasteries a large part of the lands of Walsingham had gone to the Earl of W., whose descendant is still one of the magnates of Norfolk. I had reason to believe that some books from the library had made their way to his great house at Folkham. There was no adequate catalogue of them and as I had known Lord W.'s son at Cambridge I ventured to write and ask whether I might come and look at them. His reply was very cordial. He regretted that he could not ask me to stay as the family was away and the house shut up. He had written to the housekeeper telling her to let me see anything I wanted, and added that while the only inn in the village was not to be recommended I should be sufficiently comfortable at the *Fishmongers' Arms* at Stivinghoe.

The map showed me that the distance from Stivinghoe to Folkham House was only about three miles. A bicycle would solve the question of transport. I had never slept at the *Fishmongers' Arms*, but had had tea there more than once when exploring the neighbourhood, and my recollection of it confirmed Lord W.'s opinion.

Accordingly I wrote engaging a bedroom (if possible with a table at which I could write) for a week and established myself there one fine afternoon in the middle of September.

The greater part of the next three days was spent in the library at Folkham. The result was, however, rather disappointing. The manuscripts were not many. Neither contents nor workmanship were of outstanding interest. I thought I had got to the end of them when I came upon a bundle of papers tied up with tape and docketed, in a modern hand, *Stivinghoe Chapel.*

The housekeeper had just come into the room with some tea and I noticed that she seemed to be disconcerted when she saw the bundle in my hand.

'Are these private papers, do you suppose?' I said. 'They were on the same shelf as the other manuscripts. Is there any, reason why I shouldn't read them? I see that somebody had them out not very long ago.'

'Yes, Sir,' she said. 'That were his lordship's father, that were. The day before the great storm, not that that had anything to do with it, I do suppose. No, I don't see there'd be no harm--if so be as you're careful, Sir.'

Of course I told her that I would take great care of them, that I was accustomed to handling old books and papers and so forth. But I couldn't help thinking that that was not quite what she meant.

It was too late to do any more that day. So I said I would come back and go through them to-morrow morning.

I mounted my bicycle at the front door expecting to enjoy the ride home as it was a beautiful evening. But somehow I did not. For some reason I felt uncomfortable and could not get rid of the idea that there was someone following me. Though after all why shouldn't there be on a public highroad? And what harm could he do me in broad daylight if he were evilly disposed? All the same so strong was the feeling that I looked behind me more than once. But I had the road to myself. All the same I rode faster than usual and was glad when I found myself at the *Fishmongers' Arms.*

After dinner I went into the bar-parlour as usual and got into conversation with its frequenters. The talk was of the usual description in such places. Interesting enough to anyone who, like myself, can find pleasure in listening to reminiscences of past harvests, speculations as to quality of the next one, the market prices of beasts and local affairs generally. But not worth attempting to set down here.

The company broke up early and I went early to bed. Contrary to my usual custom I did not sleep very well. I was troubled by a recurrent dream, the details of which eluded me, try as I would to recall them. The general sense was that I was going somewhere where I expected to meet, or at least feared that I might meet, somebody whom I did not want to see, Just as I was on the point of coming face to face with him I always woke up. This performance was repeated with monotonous regularity four or five times between midnight (which I heard on the church clock) and dawn. As soon as it was light I gave up trying to go to sleep and read until it was time to get up.

After breakfast I bicycled to Folkham House as usual and got out the bundle of papers.

They proved more interesting than I had expected. They belonged to the years 1531-2 and appeared to relate to the incumbent of the chapel at the end of the bank. John of Costessey was his name.

The first document was brief. It was addressed to the Prior and Convent of Walsingham and was a request bearing about a dozen signatures, of which three seemed to be those of the rectors of Stivinghoe and two neighbouring villages, that John might be recalled to Walsingham and someone else despatched to take his place.

Presumably the Prior wrote, as he was bound to do, to ask the reason for this request, for the next letter was considerably longer. It appeared that John was suspected of having entered into a compact with the powers of evil. He was a man of violent and vindictive temper and it was noticeable that those who offended him were dogged by persistent and inexplicable misfortune. Next time they went to sea they met with no fish; or nets broke mysteriously as a catch was being brought on board. Unaccountable accidents, some fatal, occurred on board their boats. More than once a boat had been lost with all hands in a sudden and very violent storm, which had not been foreseen by the most weather-wise seamen along the coast.

More than once he had been seen from boats rounding the end of the bank close inshore to make the harbour, standing at the water's edge with an imp seated on his shoulder. The said imp had screamed and waved its arms [here followed an illegible word which I guessed to be meant for *devilishly*].

More than once at night-time the window of the Chapel had been seen, to be brightly lighted, and bursts of song were heard proceeding from it. These melodies did not suggest the familiar offices of the Church and more than one voice seemed to be taking part.

Next came a letter from John himself, obviously in answer to a communication from the Prior. He protested that he could not be expected to reply in detail to such malicious and unfounded charges (*crimina tam perfida ac dolosa et omnino nugatoria*) and hinted that if his nocturnal vigils had been solaced by celestial company no fault could be found with him on that score (*quid in hoc improperii vel quae increpationis causa*?).

The Prior's answer to this may be inferred to have been a summons to repair to Walsingham forthwith. John's next letter was to the effect that his austerities, which it was his delight to practise, had made him too feeble to undertake the journey on foot, while the hard-heartedness and irreligion of the countryside, of which the Prior had had ample proof (*litteris supradictis satis probatum*), made it unlikely that any attempt to borrow so much as an ass would be successful.

The Prior could hardly be expected to put up with this, nor did he. He must have told John that he proposed to visit him in person, for the last letter was as follows:

Quamquam in rebus humus vitae delectari non fas, attamen cum hic viderim oculis meis sanctissimum Priorem una cum duo bus fratribus dilectissimis libenter dicam Domine nunc dimittis servum tuum, etc.

(Although we are forbidden to take pleasure in the things of this life, yet when I have seen here with my eyes the most holy Prior together with two of my dearly beloved brethren I shall gladly say, 'Lord, now lettest thou Thy servant depart,' etc.)

'Well,' I said to myself, 'he may have been an impudent rascal if nothing worse. But he seems to have had a sense of humour and to have been pretty sure of his ground. I wonder how the story ended?'

Next moment I gave a violent start, for I heard what sounded like a laugh close behind me. I whipped round in my chair. But there was no one there. The library was a large room and I was some distance from the door. Although the carpet was thick I did not think anyone could have come in without my knowledge. However, I got up, and went all round the room and even looked behind the window curtains. Of course I found nobody, and sat down again feeling rather ashamed of myself for being so fanciful.

There was only one more paper to be examined. Unfortunately the top had been torn off and the first words remaining were *nusquan inveniri potuit* (could not be found anywhere).

Then followed an inventory of the contents of the Chapel and cell. The only unusual item was *Duae cerae nigrae* (Two candles of black wax).

I concluded that the Prior had paid his visit, but that John's nerve had failed him at the last moment and he had disappeared. He could have made his way to Lynn without much difficulty and got on board a ship bound for the Low Countries.

No doubt the Prior was not sorry to be rid of him, and as the inventory was dated Festo S. Edithae MDXXXII (16 September 1532) the convent soon had other things to think about.

On my way home I speculated, not for the first time, upon the question whether there is or can be any foundation for any of the stories of compacts between human beings and evil spirits. In the abstract the possibility seems difficult to dispute. The belief is ancient and widely diffused. The real point seems to be whether the game could be worth the candle.

As I had finished all I meant to do at Folkham House I decided that I would spend to-morrow on a visit to the Chapel and perhaps sketch it. The day after I would return home.

When I imparted my plan to the landlord he naturally expressed a civil regret that my stay at Stivinghoe was coming to an end. He seemed doubtful whether the ruins (as I had learned the Chapel was called locally) were worth visiting, seeing as it were a dull trudge along the bank to get there. I thought from his manner that that was not his only reason for trying to discourage me. But he was summoned elsewhere before he had time to say more. While I was at dinner he looked in to see if I had everything I wanted. This was an unusual piece of condescension and I suspected an ulterior motive of some sort. I was not mistaken. After a moment or two he made an obvious effort.

'You'll excuse me, Sir. But the ruins is a queer place. Rare goings on there in those ancient times--by what I've heard.'

This was interesting as it suggested that some reminiscence of John of Costessey lingered on the scene of his activities. But before I could ask for details he went on rapidly, 'Not that I've any call to listen to the fishermen's talk--no more than what you 'ave.'

After this there was obviously no more to be got out of him. But I thought I would try a cast among the company in the parlour later on. After some miscellaneous conversation I mentioned that I thought of spending my last day in walking out along the bank and making a sketch of the ruins. For some reason the company seemed to find this proposal disturbing. No one made any comment but there was an awkward pause. Then two ancients near the fireplace held a short muttered conversation. The only words I could catch sounded like 'not lately, have he?'

Plainly they knew more than they meant to tell. Presently someone introduced some ordinary topic, and conversation flowed easily as before.

I went to bed about eleven and slept soundly.

Next morning I started soon after breakfast. I had ascertained that the tide would be low between 1 and 2 p.m. so that I should be able to find a position from which to make a sketch. I could hardly do this if I were confined to the bank itself. Also the day, though fine, was windy; windy enough, I thought, to make the top of the bank a wet place at high water.

I asked for some sandwiches to take with me and said that I should be back in time for dinner as usual, probably for tea. I thought the landlord looked at me rather reproachfully, but he said nothing When I had gone a few steps on my way I found that I had not filled my tobacco pouch that morning. I turned back to make the omission good and my eye was caught by a horseshoe nailed over the front door. Nothing remarkable in that, you may say, but I wondered that I had not noticed it before, as it now seemed to be unusually conspicuous.

The walk along the bank was pleasant enough. I could see over miles of marsh on either hand. Inland there were groups of red-roofed cottages to be seen, with occasional windmills and church towers. In front of me lay the sea. At the moment no fishing-boats were visible, but the smoke of one or two large ships could be seen on the horizon.

Altogether an exhilarating prospect. But somehow or other I did not feel at all exhilarated. On the contrary I had to admit that I was nervous and depressed.

Certainly I had had some odd little experiences since I had touched the Stivinghoe papers, First there was the feeling that I was being followed on the way home. Then my uncomfortable and inconclusive dream. Then the laugh which I thought (no, *knew*) that I had heard in the library; and last of all the obvious conviction of the neighbourhood that the ruins were better left alone. What should I do if I saw a figure emerge from the Chapel and come along the bank to meet me? Should I enter into conversation or should I get down on to the sand and hope that he would pass me by? Or should I run for it? Or could I recall on the spur of the moment any form of exorcism which might prove effective? Fortunately I did not have to answer any of these questions.

The Chapel was a small building, roughly built of grey flint. It measured about twenty-two feet by ten and was lighted by a single lancet in the east wall. There was a door at the west end, I put its date at a little before 1350. Of course the roof was gone, but the walls looked fairly sound. The altar was still in place. But I noticed that the usual consecration crosses (one in the middle and one at each corner) had been deliberately obliterated. The chisel marks could be seen clearly. Such reforming zeal seemed to be almost excessive.

On the south (that is on the landward) side of the Chapel there were some small mounds which presumably indicated the site of the priest's dwelling. The superstructure had disappeared so completely that I wondered whether it had been of wood; also whether it could possibly be worth while to return with a spade.

I sat down on one of the mounds and ate my sandwiches. Then I thought it time to set about my sketch. I went down on to the sand and decided that the best position was a few yards to seaward. (In this part of Norfolk the coast runs east and west, so that the sea is to the north. The natives are fond of assuring visitors that there is nothing between them and the North Pole. No one who has been there in winter is likely to wish to dispute this statement.) The tide was still ebbing, so I should have plenty of time to do what I wanted.

I settled myself and my sketching materials, but somehow I did not make very good progress. I had an uncomfortable feeling, as if there was somebody behind me, and caught myself wondering what I should do if a hand (probably a large and bony one) were suddenly laid upon my shoulder. I said aloud 'ridiculous' and as I did so a gull passed very close above my head and gave a derisive squawk, which seemed to indicate his complete concurrence.

The gulls were very many; which was not surprising. But they were so tame (or impudent, whichever you like to call it) that they were a positive nuisance. They flapped their wings almost in my face and one actually perched on my easel. I suppose they had never seen enough of men to be afraid of them. I had a sandwich or two left which I threw as far as I could towards the water's edge. This drew them off for a little, but they were soon as bad as ever. However, I got a sketch of some sort finished. I thought I would take one more look inside the Chapel before I started to walk home in case there were any detail of interest which I had missed. The floor was covered with coarse turf. Probably it had never been paved; if it had, the paving had been covered long since. But just in front of the altar I noticed a patch which somehow looked different from the rest. I had in my knife one of those curious implements said to be intended for taking stones out of horses' feet, and it seemed that at last I had a chance of using it. I scratched at the turf and very soon my hook grated upon a stone. A little scraping disclosed a small rectangular slab about twenty inches long by eight broad. A pentacle had been scratched upon it rather roughly. It was obviously the lid of something, if it were too small for any kind of coffin. A little more scraping of the earth round its edges and I got it up with less difficulty than I had expected. It was the lid of a coffin of sorts after all and in the coffin were some bones; clearly those of a small monkey. Its forepaws were crossed upon its breast and from some fragments of stuff which lay about I came to the conclusion that it had been buried in some sort of monastic habit.

This discovery explained the stories of the imp. Perhaps John had been really fond of his pet who must have been his only companion. Burial before the altar might perhaps be condoned. But the monastic habit looked like a profane jest. Or was it more than a jest? Taken in conjunction with the pentacle on the lid, the candles of black wax found by the Prior and the erasure of the consecration crosses (which I now began to think was John's handiwork and not the doing of any zealous follower of Dowsing) there was a definite suggestion of serious and sinister purpose. What unhallowed rites had been celebrated there, with what evil intent? And (I could not repress the, further question) in what company?

However, there seemed to be nothing for me to do but to leave things as I had found them. Which I did. The afternoon was wearing on, so I started for home. The tide had probably turned but was still very low. At the seaward end the line of the bank was curved, so I saw that I could shorten my walk considerably if I took to the sands and struck the bank again in about a mile. When I had gone a little way I turned to take a final look at the Chapel. It was a sunny day with big white clouds driving before the wind. As I looked the shadow of one passed across the Chapel, and by some odd trick of light made it seem as if a dark figure had emerged from the door and dropped down the far side of the bank. For a moment I was really startled.

I turned and went on with my walk. I have never considered myself a fanciful person, but it was borne in upon me very forcibly that the sooner I was sitting down to tea at the *Fishmongers' Arms* the happier I should be.

Presently I reached the point at which I must take to the bank again. Just as I got to the edge of the sand I saw the print of a naked human foot, pointing towards the bank. It was very recent and could (apparently) only have been made by someone who had passed me quite close, having come across the sand as I had, and gone up the bank before me. This was frankly impossible. Had there been anyone else about I could not have failed to see him. The sand was too wet to hold impressions for long. Most of my own tracks had disappeared already. Yet there was the footprint, unmistakably. I stooped and looked at it (there was only one, which made it odder still) closely. It struck me as unusually bony, that is to say, the bones showed more plainly than I should have expected. I thought of the shadow which I had seen pass across the end of the Chapel. Had it, after all, emerged from the inside? If I went on, should I find someone waiting for me, and with what intent? However, there was nothing for it but to go on. I was within sight of the village now and there were people about who would see if any attack were made upon me, though what help they would be able to give was another matter. So on I went, and in a few minutes had reached my inn safely.

I turned on the doorstep to take a look over the marshes. Very lonely and solemn they were and very dark was the little Chapel. There was no one to be seen; I had not expected that there would be.

By this time the wind had freshened and there was a hard brightness on the northeastern horizon which foretold a full gale before morning. There was an old barometer just inside the front door which had fallen so low that I wondered whether it were trustworthy and hoped not. The landlord emerged and appeared ill at ease, and at the same time glad to see me--possibly by reason of the weather; possibly not. He murmured something to the effect of no harm done, as he returned to his occupations. I felt curiously tired, and when I had had tea, after a poor pretence of reading some book (I forget now what) dozed in an armchair by the fire.

I was roused by a clap of thunder and the storm broke with a roar like a train. The thunder was unusual, I thought, for the time of year, especially as the last few days had not been particularly hot. Also, the wind was off the sea, and I knew that there was a belief along the coast that when a thunderstorm comes up from the sea, that will be the beginning of the end of the world.

The *Fishmongers' Arms* was built to stand weather. But I doubt whether it ever had a worse buffeting than it got that night. There was no more thunder, but the rain came down in sheets and the wind tore at the house till I could almost imagine I felt it swaying to and fro. It was obvious that there would be no customers at the bar, so after dinner I invited the landlord to come to my sitting-room to smoke a cigar and drink a whisky and soda with me. I was really glad of his company, and he seemed to be of mine. We tried to talk of indifferent subjects, but could not do much save listen to the wind. We went to bed about eleven, though there was not much prospect of sleep. I wished that I had not remembered at that moment that Richard Kidder, Bishop of Bath and Wells, had been killed in his bed, together with his wife, by the fall of a chimney-stack through the roof of the palace during the terrible storm of 26-7 November, 1703.

Soon after midnight there was a screech (I can call it nothing else) like that of an animal in pain. I could hardly have believed that the wind could have made such a sound. This seemed to be its last effort, and the storm died away almost as quickly as it had arisen.

When I looked out next morning the Chapel was gone. The whole end of the bank had been washed away. The gale had coincided with a spring tide and I suspect that most of the marsh had been under water for some hours. Of course the tip of the bank had caught the full force of the sea.

I must confess that I felt relieved At first I was glad that I had made a sketch of the Chapel. But after a little reflection I burned it. Somehow I felt safer as I saw it turn to ashes.

THE SUNDIAL

The following story came into my hands by pure chance. I had wandered into a second-hand book-shop in the neighbourhood of the Charing Cross Road and was about to leave it empty-handed. On a shelf near the door my eye fell upon a copy of Hacket's *Scrinia Reserata* solidly bound in leather, which I thought well worth the few shillings which the proprietor was willing to accept for it. It is not an easy book to come by, and is of real value to anyone who wants to understand certain aspects of English Church History during the first half of the seventeenth century.

When I opened the book at home a thickish wad of paper fell out. It proved to consist of several sheets of foolscap covered with writing. I have reproduced the contents word for word.

From the look of the paper I judged that it had been there for at least thirty years. The author had not signed it, and there was nothing to indicate to whom the book had belonged. I think I could make a guess at the neighbourhood to which the story relates, and if I am right it should not be difficult to identify the house and discover the name of the tenant. But as he seems to have wished to remain anonymous he shall do so, as far as I am concerned.

The form of the story suggests that he intended to publish it; probably in some magazine. As far as I know it has not been printed before.

I belong to one of the numerous middle-class English families which for several generations have followed various professions, with credit, but without ever attaining any very special distinction. In our own case India could almost claim us as hereditary bondsmen. For more than a century most of our men had made their way there, and had served John Company or the Crown in various capacities. One of my uncles had risen to be Legal Member of the Viceroy's Council. So when my own time came, to India I went--in the Civil Service--and there I lived for five and twenty years.

My career was neither more nor less adventurous than the average. The routine of my work was occasionally broken by experiences which would sound incredible to an English reader, and therefore need not be set down here. Just before the time came for my retirement a legacy made me a good deal better off than I had had any reason to expect to be. So upon my return to England I found that it would be possible for me to adopt the life of a country gentleman, upon a modest scale, but with the prospect of finding sufficient occupation and amusement.

I was never married, and had been too long out of England to have any very strong ties remaining. I was free to establish myself where I pleased, and the advertisements in the *Field* and *Country Life* offered houses of every description in every part of the kingdom. After much correspondence, and some fruitless journeys, I came upon one which seemed to satisfy my requirements. It lay about sixty miles north of London upon a main line of railway. That was an important point, as I was a Fellow of both the Asiatic and Historical Societies, and had long looked forward to attending their meetings regularly. As a boy I had known the neighbourhood slightly and had liked it, though it is not generally considered beautiful. There were two packs of hounds within reach, which could be followed with such a stable as I should be able to afford.

The house was an old one. It had been a good deal larger, but part had been battered down during the Civil War, when it was besieged by the Parliamentary troops, and never rebuilt. It belonged to one of the largest landowners in the county, whom I will call Lord Rye. It generally served as the dower-house of the family, but as there was at that moment no dowager Countess, and as Lord Rye himself was a young man, and both his sisters were married, it was not likely to be wanted for some time to come. It had been unoccupied for nearly two years. The last tenant, a retired doctor, had been found dead on the lawn at the bottom of the steps leading up to the garden door. His heart had been in a bad condition for some time past, so that his sudden death was not surprising; but the neighbouring village viewed the incident with some suspicion. One or two of the older people professed to remember traditions of 'trouble' there in former years.

This had made it difficult to get a caretaker, and as Lord Rye was anxious to let again he was willing to take an almost nominal rent. In fact his whole attitude suggested that I was doing him a favour by becoming his tenant. About five hundred acres of shooting generally went with the house, and I was glad to find that I could have them very cheaply.

I moved in at midsummer, and each day made me more and more pleased with my new surroundings.

After my years in India the garden was a particular source of delight to me; but I will not describe it more minutely than is necessary to make what follows intelligible. Behind the house was a good-sized lawn, flanked by shrubbery. On the far side, parallel with the house, ran a splendid yew hedge, nearly fifteen feet high and very thick. It came up to the shrubbery at either end, but was pierced by two archways about thirty yards apart, giving access to the flower-garden beyond. Almost in the middle of the lawn was an old tree stump, or what looked like one, some three feet high. Though covered with ivy it was not picturesque, and I told Lord Rye that I should like to take it up. 'Do by all means,' he said, 'I certainly should if I lived here. I believe poor Riley (the last tenant) intended to put a sundial there. I think it would look rather nice, don't you?'

This struck me as a good idea. I ordered a sundial from a well-known firm of heliological experts in Cockspur Street, and ordered the stump to be grubbed up as soon as it arrived.

One morning towards the end of September I woke unrefreshed after a night of troubled dreams. I could not recall them very distinctly, but I had seemed to be trying to lift a very heavy weight of some kind from the ground. But, before I could raise it, an overwhelming terror had taken hold of me--though I could not remember why--and I woke to find my forehead wet with perspiration. Each time I fell asleep again the dream repeated itself with mechanical regularity, though the details did not become any more distinct. So I was heartily glad it had become late enough to get up. The day was wet and chilly. I felt tired and unwell, and was, moreover, depressed by a vague sense of impending disaster. This was accentuated by a feeling that it lay within my power to avert the catastrophe, if only I could discover what it was.

In the afternoon the weather cleared, and I thought that a ride would do me good. I rode fairly hard for some distance, and it was past five o'clock before I had reached my own bounds'-ditch on my way home. At that particular place a small wood ran along the edge of my property for about a quarter of a mile. I was riding slowly down the outside, and was perhaps a hundred yards from the angle where I meant to turn it, when I noticed a man standing at the corner. The light was beginning to fail, and he was so close to the edge of the wood that at first I could not be sure whether it was a human figure, or only an oddly shaped tree-stump which I had never noticed before. But when I got a little nearer I saw that my first impression had been correct, and that it was a man. He seemed to be dressed like an ordinary agricultural labourer. He was standing absolutely still and seemed to be looking very intently in my direction. But he was shading his eyes with his hand, so that I could not make out his face. Before I had got close enough to make him out more definitely he turned suddenly and vanished round the corner of the wood. His movements were rapid: but he somehow gave the impression of being deformed, though in what precise respect I could not tell. Naturally my suspicions were stirred, so I put my horse to a canter. But when we had reached the corner he shied violently, and I had some difficulty in getting him to pass it. When we had got round, the mysterious man was nowhere to be seen. In front and on the left hand lay a very large stubble field, without a vestige of cover of any kind. I could see that he was not crossing it, and unless he had flown he could not have reached the other side.

On the right hand lay the ditch bounding the wood. As is usual in that country it was both wide and deep, and had some two or three feet of mud and water at the bottom. If the man had gone that way he had some very pressing reason for wishing to avoid me: and I could detect no trace of his passage at any point.

So there was nothing to be done but go home, and tell the policeman next day to keep his eyes open for any suspicious strangers. However, no attempts were made upon any of my belongings, and when October came my pheasants did not seem to have been unlawfully diminished.

October that year was stormy, and one Saturday night about the middle of the month it blew a regular gale. I lay awake long listening to the wind, and to all the confused sounds which fill an old house in stormy weather. Twice I seemed to hear footsteps in the passage. Once I could have almost sworn my door was cautiously opened and closed again. When at last I dropped off I was disturbed by a repetition of my former dream. But this time the details were rather more distinct. Again I was trying to lift a heavy weight from the ground: but now I knew that there was something hidden under it. What the concealed object might be I could not tell, but as I worked to bring it to light a feeling began to creep over me that I did not want to see it. This soon deepened into horror at the bare idea of seeing it: though I had still no notion what manner of thing it might be. Yet I could not abandon my task. So presently I found myself in the position of working hard to accomplish what I would have given the world to have left undone. At this point I woke, to find myself shaking with fright, and repeating aloud the apparently meaningless sentence--'If you'll pull, I'll push.'

I did not sleep for the rest of that night. Beside the noise of the storm the prospect of a repetition of that dream was quite enough to keep me awake. To add to my discomfort a verse from Ecclesiastes ran in my head with dismal persistence--'But if a man live many years and rejoice in them all, yet let him remember the days of darkness, for they shall be many.' Days of darkness seemed to be coming upon me now, and my mind was filled with vague alarm.

The next day was fine, and after Church I thought I would see how my fruit trees had fared during the night. The kitchen-garden was enclosed by a high brick wall. On the side nearest the house there were two doors, which were always kept locked on Sunday. In the wall opposite was a trap-door, about three feet square, giving on to a rather untidy piece of ground, partly orchard and partly waste. When I had unlocked the door I saw standing by the opposite wall the figure which I had seen at the corner of the wood. His neck was abnormally long, and so malformed that his head lolled sideways on to his right shoulder in a disgusting and almost inhuman fashion. He was bent almost double; and I think he was misshapen in some other respect as well. But of that I could not be certain. He raised his hand with what seemed to be a threatening gesture, then turned, and slipped through the trap-door with remarkable quickness. I was after him immediately, but on reaching the opposite wall received a shock which stopped me like a physical blow. The trap-door was shut and bolted on the inside. I tried to persuade myself that a violent slam might make the bolts shoot, but I knew that that was really impossible. I had to choose between two explanations. Either my visitor was a complete hallucination, or else he possessed the unusual power of being able to bolt a door upon the side on which he himself was not. The latter was upon the whole the more comforting, and--in view of some of my Indian experiences--the more probable, supposition.

After a little hesitation I opened the trap and, as there was nothing to be seen, got through it and went up to the top of the orchard, where the kennels lay. But neither of my dogs would follow the scent. When brought to the spot where his feet must have touched the ground they whined and showed every symptom of alarm. When I let go of their collars they hurried home in a way which showed plainly what they thought of the matter.

This seemed to dispose of the idea of hallucination, and, as before, there was nothing else to be done but await developments as patiently as I could. For the next fortnight nothing remarkable took place. I had my usual health and as near an approach to my usual spirits as could reasonably be expected. I had visitors for part of the time, but no one to whom I should have cared to confide the story at this stage. I was not molested further by day, and my dreams, though varied, were not alarming.

On the morning of the 31st I received a letter announcing that my sundial had been despatched, and it duly arrived in the course of the afternoon. It was heavy, so by the time we had got it out of the railway van and on to the lawn it was too late to place it in position that day. The men departed to drink my health, and I turned towards the house. Just as I reached the door I paused. A sensation--familiar to all men who are much alone--had come over me, and I felt as if I were being watched from behind. Usually the feeling can be dispelled by turning round. I did so, but on this occasion the sense that I was not alone merely increased. Of course the lawn was deserted, but I stood looking across it for a few moments, telling myself that I must not let my nerves play me tricks. Then I saw a face detach itself slowly from the darkness of the hedge at one side of the left-hand arch. For a few seconds it hung, horribly poised, in the middle of the opening like a mask suspended by an invisible thread. Then the body to which it belonged slid into the clear space, and I saw my acquaintance of the wood and kitchen-garden, this time sharply outlined against a saffron sky. There could be no mistaking his bowed form and distorted neck, but now his appearance was made additionally abominable by his expression. The yellow sunset light seemed to stream all round him, and showed me features convulsed with fury. He gnashed his teeth and clawed the air with both hands. I have never seen such a picture of impotent rage.

It was more by instinct than by any deliberate courage that I ran straight across the lawn towards him. He was gone in a flash, and when I came through the archway where he had stood he was hurrying down the side of the hedge towards the other. He moved with an odd shuffling gait, and I made sure that I should soon overtake him. But to my surprise I found that I did not gain much. His limping shuffle took him over the ground as fast as I could cover it. In fact, when I reached the point from which I had started I thought I had actually lost a little. When we came round for the second time there was no doubt about it. This was humiliating, but I persevered, relying now on superior stamina. But during the third circuit it suddenly flashed upon me that our positions had become reversed. I was no longer the pursuer. He--it----whatever the creature was, was now chasing me, and the distance between us was diminishing rapidly.

I am not ashamed to admit that my nerve failed completely. I believe I screamed aloud. I ran on stumblingly, helplessly, as one runs in a dream, knowing now that the creature behind was gaining at every stride. How long the chase lasted I do not know, but presently I could hear his irregular footstep close behind me, and a horrible dank breath played about the back of my neck. We were on the side towards the house when I looked up and saw my butler standing at the garden door, with a note in his hand. The sight of his prosaic form seemed to break the spell which had kept me running blindly round and round the hedge. I was almost exhausted, but I tore across the lawn, and fell in a heap at the bottom of the steps.

Parker was an ex-sergeant of Marines, which amounts to saying that he was incapable of surprise and qualified to cope with any practical emergency which could arise. He picked me up, helped me into the house, gave me a tumbler of brandy diluted with soda-water, and fortified himself with another, without saying a word. How much he saw, or what he thought of it, I could never learn, for all subsequent approaches to the question were parried with the evasive skill which seems to be the birthright of all them that go down to the sea in ships. But his general view of the situation is indicated by the fact that he sent for the Rector, not the doctor, and--as I learned afterwards--had a private conference with him before he left the house. Soon afterwards he joined the choir--or in his own phrase 'assisted with the singing in the chancel'--and for many months the village church had no more regular or vocal attendant.

The Rector heard my story gravely, and was by no means disposed to make light of it. Something similar had come his way once before, when he had had the charge of a parish on the Northumbrian Border. He was confident, he said, that no harm could come to me that night, if I remained indoors, and departed to look up some of his authorities on such subjects.

That night was noisy with wind, so the insistent knocking which I seemed to hear during the small hours at the garden-door and ground-floor windows, which were secured with outside shutters, may have had no existence outside my imagination. I had asked Parker to occupy a dressing-room opening out of my bedroom for the night. He seemed very ready to do so, but I do not think that he slept very much either. Early next morning the Rector reappeared, saying that he thought he had got a clue, though it was impossible to say yet how much it might be worth. He had brought with him the first volume of the parish register, and showed me the following note on the inside of the cover:

'October 31st, 1578. On this day Jn. Croxton a Poore Man hanged himself from a Beame within his House. He was a very stubborn Popish Recusant and ye manner of his Death was in accord with his whole Life. He was buried that evening at ye Cross Roades.'

'It is unfortunate,' continued the Rector, 'that we have no sixteenth-century map of the parish. But there is a map of 1759 which marks a hamlet at the cross-roads just outside your gate. The hamlet doesn't exist now--you know that the population hereabouts is much less than it used to be--but it used to be called New Cross. I think that must mean that these particular cross-roads are comparatively recent. Now this house is known to have been built between 1596 and 1602. The straight way from Farley to Abbotsholme would lie nearly across its site. I think, therefore, that the Elizabethan Lord Rye diverted the old road when he laid out his grounds. That would also account for the loop which the present road makes'--here he traced its course with his finger on the map which he had brought.

'Now I strongly suspect that your visitor was Mr. Croxton, and that he is buried somewhere in your grounds. If we could find the place I think we could keep him quiet for the future. But I am afraid that there is nothing to guide us.'

At this point Parker came in. 'Beg your pardon, Sir, but Hardman is wishful to speak to you. About that there bollard on the quarter-deck, Sir--stump on the lawn, I should have said, Sir--what you told him to put over the side.'

We went out, and found Hardman and the boy looking at a large hole in the lawn. By the side of it lay what we had taken for a tree stump. But it had never struck root there. It was a very solid wooden stake, some nine feet in length over all, with a sharp point. It had been driven some six feet into the ground, passing through a layer of rubble about three feet from the surface. At the bottom the hole widened, forming a large, and plainly artificial, cavity. The earth here looked as if it had been recently disturbed, but the condition of the stake showed that that was impossible. It was obvious to both of us that we had come upon Mr. Croxton's grave, at the original cross-roads, and that what had appeared to be a natural stump was really the stake which had been driven through it to keep him there. We did not, of course, take the gardeners into our confidence, but told them to leave the place for the present as it might contain some interesting antiques--presumably Roman--which we would get out carefully with our own hands.

We soon enlarged the shaft sufficiently to explore the cavity at the bottom. We had naturally expected to find a skeleton, or something of the sort, there, but we were disappointed. We could not discover the slightest vestige of bones or body, or of any dust except that of natural soil. Once while we were working we were startled by a harsh sound like the cry of a night-jar, apparently very close at hand. But whatever it was passed away very quickly, as if the creature which had made it was on the wing, and it was not repeated.

By the Rector's advice we went to the churchyard and brought away sufficient consecrated earth to fill up the cavity. The shaft was filled up, and the sundial securely planted on top of it. The pious mottoes with which it was adorned, according to custom, assumed for the first time a practical significance.

'It not infrequently happens,' said the Rector, 'that those who for any reason have not received full Christian Burial are unable, or unwilling, to remain quiet in their graves, particularly if the interment has been at all carelessly carried out in the first instance. They seem to be particularly active on or about the anniversary of their death in any year. The range of their activities is varied, and it would be difficult to define the nature of the power which animates them, or the source from which it is derived. But I incline to think that it is less their own personality than some force inherent in the earth itself, of which they become the vehicle. With the exception of Vampires (who are altogether *sui generis* and virtually unknown in this country), they can seldom do much direct physical harm. They operate indirectly by terrifying, but are commonly compelled to stop there. But it is always necessary for them to have free access to their graves. If that is obstructed in any way their power seems to lapse. That is why I think that their vitality is in some way bred of the earth: and I am sure that you won't be troubled with any more visits now.

'Our friend was afraid that your sundial would interfere with his convenience, and I think he was trying to frighten you into leaving the house. Of course, if your heart had been weak he might have disposed of you as he did of your unfortunate predecessor. His projection of himself into your dreams was part of his general plan: I incline to think, however, that it was an error of judgment, as it might have put you on your guard. But I very much doubt whether he could have inflicted any physical injury on you if he had caught you yesterday afternoon.'

'H'm,' said I, 'you might be right there. But I am very glad that I shall never know.'

Next day Parker asked for leave to go to London. He returned with a large picture representing King Solomon issuing directions to a corvée of demons of repellent aspect whom he had (according to a well-known Jewish legend) compelled to labour at the building of the Temple. This he proceeded to affix with drawing-pins to the inside of the pantry door. He called my attention to it particularly, and said that he had got it from a Jew whom he had known in Malta, who had recently opened a branch establishment in the Whitechapel Road. I ventured to make some comment on the singularity of the subject, but Parker was, as usual, impenetrable. 'Beggin' your pardon, Sir,' he said, 'there's some things what a civilian don't never 'ave no chance of learnin', not even if 'e 'ad the brains for it. I done my twenty-one years in the Service--*in puris naturalibus* all the time as the saying is--and' (pointing to the figure of the King) you may lay to it that that there man knew 'is business.'

BETWEEN SUNSET AND MOONRISE

During the early part of last year it fell to me to act as executor for an old friend. We had not seen much of each other of late, as he had been living in the west of England, and my own time had been fully occupied elsewhere. The time of our intimacy had been when he was vicar of a large parish not very far from Cambridge. I will call it Yaxholme, though that is not its name.

The place had seemed to suit him thoroughly. He had been on the best of terms with his parishioners, and with the few gentry of the neighbourhood. The church demanded a custodian of antiquarian knowledge and artistic perception, and in these respects too my friend was particularly well qualified for his position. But a sudden nervous breakdown had compelled him to resign. The cause of it had always been a mystery to his friends, for he was barely middle-aged when it took place, and had been a man of robust health. His parish was neither particularly laborious nor harassing; and, as far as was known, he had no special private anxieties of any kind. But the collapse came with startling suddenness, and was so severe that, for a time, his reason seemed to be in danger. Two years of rest and travel enabled him to lead a normal life again, but he was never the man he had been. He never revisited his old parish, or any of his friends in the county; and seemed to be ill at ease if conversation turned upon the part of England in which it lay. It was perhaps not unnatural that he should dislike the place which had cost him so much. But his friends could not but regard as childish the length to which he carried his aversion.

He had had a distinguished career at the University, and had kept up his intellectual interests in later life. But, except for an occasional *succès d'estime* in a learned periodical, he had published nothing. I was not without hope of finding something completed among his papers which would secure for him a permanent lace in the world of learning. But in this I was disappointed. His literary remains were copious, and a striking testimony to the vigour and range of his intellect. But they were very fragmentary. There was nothing which could be made fit for publication, except one document which I should have preferred to suppress. But he had left particular instructions in his will that it was to be published when he had been dead for a year. Accordingly I subjoin it exactly as it left his hand. It was dated two years after he had left Yaxholme, and nearly five before his death. For reasons which will be apparent to the reader I make no comment of any kind upon it.

The solicitude which my friends have displayed during my illness has placed me under obligations which I cannot hope to repay. But I feel that I owe it to them to explain the real cause of my breakdown. I have never spoken of it to anyone, for, had I done so, it would have been impossible to avoid questions which I should not wish to be able to answer. Though I have only just reached middle-age I am sure that I have not many more years to live. And I am therefore confident that most of my friends will survive me, and be able to hear my explanation after my death. Nothing but a lively sense of what I owe to them could have enabled me to undergo the pain of recalling the experience which I am now about to set down.

Yaxholme lies, as they will remember, upon the extreme edge of the Fen district. In shape it is a long oval, with a main line of railway cutting one end. The church and vicarage were close to the station, and round them lay a village containing nearly five-sixths of the entire population of the parish. On the other side of the line the Fen proper began, and stretched for many miles. Though it is now fertile corn land, much of it had been permanently under water within living memory, and would soon revert to its original condition if it were not for the pumping stations. In spite of these it is not unusual to see several hundred acres flooded in winter.

My own parish ran for nearly six miles, and I had therefore several scattered farms and cottages so far from the village that a visit to one of them took up the whole of a long afternoon. Most of them were not on any road, and could only be reached by means of droves. For the benefit of those who are not acquainted with the Fen I may explain that a drove is a very imperfect sketch of the idea of a road. It is bounded by hedges or dykes, so that the traveller cannot actually lose his way, but it offers no further assistance to his progress. The middle is simply a grass track, and as cattle have to be driven along it the mud is sometimes literally knee-deep in winter. In summer the light peaty soil rises in clouds of sable dust. In fact I seldom went down one without recalling Hesiod's unpatriotic description of his native village in Bœotia. 'Bad in winter; intolerable in summer; good at no time.'

At the far end of one of these lay a straggling group of half a dozen cottages, of which the most remote was inhabited by an old woman whom I will call Mrs. Vries. In some ways she was the most interesting of all my parishioners, and she was certainly the most perplexing. She was not a native, but had come to live there some twenty years before, and it was hard to see what had tempted a stranger to so unattractive a spot. It was the last house in the parish: her nearest neighbour was a quarter of a mile away, and she was fully three miles from a hard road or a shop. The house itself was not at all a good one. It had been unoccupied, I was told, for some years before she came to it, and she had found it in a semi-ruinous condition. Yet she had not been driven to seek a very cheap dwelling by poverty, as she had a good supply of furniture of very good quality, and, apparently, as much money as she required. She never gave the slightest hint as to where she had come from, or what her previous history had been. As far as was known she never wrote or received any letters. She must have been between fifty and sixty when she came. Her appearance was striking, as she was tall and thin, with an aquiline nose, and a pair of very brilliant dark eyes, and a quantity of hair--snowwhite by the time I knew her. At one time she must have been handsome; but she had grown rather forbidding, and I used to think that, a couple of centuries before, she might have had some difficulty in proving that she was not a witch. Though her neighbours, not unnaturally, fought rather shy of her, her conversation showed that she was a clever woman who had at some time received a good deal of education, and had lived in cultivated surroundings. I used to think that she must have been an upper servant--most probably lady's maid--in a good house, and, despite the ring on her finger, suspected that the 'Mrs.' was brevet rank.

One New Year's Eve I thought it my duty to visit her. I had not seen her for some months, and a few days of frost had made the drove more passable than it had been for several weeks. But, in spite of her interesting personality, I always found that it required a considerable moral effort to call at her cottage. She was always civil, and expressed herself pleased to see me. But I could never get rid of the idea that she regarded civility to me in the light of an insurance, which might be claimed elsewhere. I always told myself that such thoughts were unfounded and unworthy, but I could never repress them altogether, and whenever I left her cottage it was with a strong feeling that I had no desire to see her again. I used, however, to say to myself that that was really due to personal pique (because I could never discover that she had any religion, nor could I instil any into her), and that the fault was therefore more mine than hers.

On this particular afternoon the prospect of seeing her seemed more than usually distasteful, and my disinclination increased curiously as I made my way along the drove. So strong did it become that if any reasonable excuse for turning back had presented itself I am afraid I should have seized it. However, none did: so I held on, comforting myself with the thought that I should begin the New Year with a comfortable sense of having discharged the most unpleasant of my regular duties in a conscientious fashion.

When I reached the cottage I was a little surprised at having to knock three times, and by hearing the sound of bolts cautiously drawn back. Presently the door opened and Mrs. Vries peered out. As soon as she saw who it was she made me very welcome as usual. But it was impossible not to feel that she had been more or less expecting some other visitor, whom she was not anxious to see. However, she volunteered no statement, and I thought it better to pretend to have noticed nothing unusual. On a table in the middle of the room lay a large book in which she had obviously been reading. I was surprised to see that it was a Bible, and that it lay open at the Book of Tobit. Seeing that I had noticed it Mrs. Vries told me--with a little hesitation, I thought--that she had been reading the story of Sarah and the fiend Asmodeus. Then--the ice once broken--she plied me almost fiercely with questions. 'To what cause did I attribute Sarah's obsession, in the first instance?' 'Did the efficacy of Tobias' remedy depend upon the fact that it had been prescribed by an angel?' and much more to the same effect. Naturally my answers were rather vague, and her good manners could not conceal her disappointment. She sat silent for a minute or two, while I looked at her--not, I must confess, without some alarm, for her manner had been very strange--and then said abruptly, 'Well, will you have a cup of tea with me?' I assented gladly, for it was nearly half-past four, and it would take me nearly an hour and a half to get home. She took some time over the preparations and during the meal talked with even more fluency than usual. I could not help thinking that she was trying to make it last as long as possible.

Finally, at about half-past five, I got up and said that I must go, as I had a good many odds and ends awaiting me at home. I held out my hand, and as she took it said, 'You must let me wish you a very happy New Year.'

She stared at me for a moment, and then broke into a harsh laugh, and said, 'If wishes were horses beggars might ride. Still, I thank you for your good will. Goodbye.' About thirty yards from her house there was an elbow in the drove. When I reached it I looked back and saw that she was still standing in her doorway, with her figure sharply silhouetted against the red glow of the kitchen fire. For one instant the play of shadow made it look as if there were another, taller, figure behind her, but the illusion passed directly. I waved my hand to her and turned the corner.

It was a fine, still, starlight night. I reflected that the moon would be up before I reached home, and my walk would not be unpleasant. I had naturally been rather puzzled by Mrs. Vries' behaviour, and decided that I must see her again before long, to ascertain whether, as seemed possible, her mind were giving way.

When I had passed the other cottages of the group I noticed that the stars were disappearing, and a thick white mist was rolling up. This did not trouble me. The drove now ran straight until it joined the high-road, and there was no turn into it on either side. I had therefore no chance of losing my way, and anyone who lives in the Fens is accustomed to fogs. It soon grew very thick, and I was conscious of the slightly creepy feeling which a thick fog very commonly inspires. I had been thinking of a variety of things, in somewhat desultory fashion, when suddenly--almost as if it had been whispered into my ear--a passage from the Book of Wisdom came into my mind and refused to be dislodged. My nerves were good then, and I had often walked up a lonely drove in a fog before; but still just at that moment I should have preferred to have recalled almost anything else. For this was the extract with which my memory was pleased to present me. 'For neither did the dark recesses that held them guard them from fears, but sounds rushing down rang around them; and phantoms appeared, cheerless with unsmiling faces. And no force of fire prevailed to give them light, neither were the brightest flames of the stars strong enough to illumine that gloomy night. And in terror they deemed the things which they saw to be worse than that sight on which they could not gaze. And they lay helpless, made the sport of magic art.' (*Wisdom* xvii. 4-6).

Suddenly I heard a loud snort, as of a beast, apparently at my elbow. Naturally I jumped and stood still for a moment to avoid blundering into a stray cow, but there was nothing there. The next moment I heard what sounded exactly like a low chuckle. This was more disconcerting: but common sense soon came to my aid. I told myself that the cow must have been on the other side of the hedge and not really so close as it had seemed to be. What I had taken for a chuckle must have been the squelching of her feet in a soft place. But I must confess that I did not find this explanation as convincing as I could have wished.

I plodded on, but soon began to feel unaccountably tired. I say 'unaccountably' because I was a good walker and often covered much more ground than I had done that day.

I slackened my pace, but, as I was not out of breath, that did not relieve me. I felt as if I were wading through water up to my middle, or through very deep soft snow, and at last was fairly compelled to stop. By this time I was thoroughly uneasy, wondering what could be the matter with me. But as I had still nearly two miles to go there was nothing for it but to push on as best I might.

When I started again I saw that the fog seemed to be beginning to clear, though I could not feel a breath of air. But instead of thinning in the ordinary way it merely rolled back a little on either hand, producing an effect which I had never seen before. Along the sides of the drove lay two solid banks of white, with a narrow passage clear between them. This passage seemed to stretch for an interminable distance, and at the far end I 'perceived' a number of figures. I say advisedly 'perceived,' rather than 'saw,' for I do not know whether I saw them in the ordinary sense of the word or not. That is to say--I did not know then, and have never been able to determine since, whether it was still dark. I only know that my power of vision seemed to be independent of light or darkness. I perceived the figures, as one sees the creatures of a dream, or the mental pictures which sometimes come when one is neither quite asleep nor awake.

They were advancing rapidly in orderly fashion, almost like a body of troops. The scene recalled very vividly a picture of the Israelites marching across the Red Sea between two perpendicular walls of water, in a set of Bible pictures which I had had as a child. I suppose that I had not thought of that picture for more than thirty years, but now it leapt into my mind, and I found myself saying aloud, 'Yes: of course it must have been exactly like that. How glad I am to have seen it.'

I suppose it was the interest of making the comparison that kept me from feeling the surprise which would otherwise have been occasioned by meeting a large number of people marching down a lonely drove after dark on a raw December evening.

At first I should have said there were thirty or forty in the party, but when they had drawn a little nearer they seemed to be not more than ten or a dozen strong. A moment later I saw to my surprise that they were reduced to five or six. The advancing figures seemed to be melting into one another, something after the fashion of dissolving views. Their speed and stature increased as their numbers diminished, suggesting that the survivors had, in some horrible fashion, absorbed the personality of their companions. Now there appeared to be only three, then one solitary figure of gigantic stature rushing down the drove towards me at a fearful pace, without a sound. As he came the mist closed behind him, so that his dark figure was thrown up against a solid background of white: much as mountain climbers are said sometimes to see their own shadows upon a bank of cloud. On and on he came, until at last he towered above me and I saw his face. It has come to me once or twice since in troubled dreams, and may come again. But I am thankful that I have never had any clear picture of it in my waking moments. If I had I should be afraid for my reason. I know that the impression which it produced upon me was that of intense malignity long baffled, and now at last within reach of its desire. I believe I screamed aloud. Then after a pause, which seemed to last for hours, he broke over me like a wave. There was a rushing and a streaming all round me, and I struck out with my hands as if I were swimming. The sensation was not unlike that of rising from a deep dive: there was the same feeling of pressure and suffocation, but in this case coupled with the most intense physical loathing. The only comparison which I can suggest is that I felt as a man might feel if he were buried under a heap of worms or toads.

Suddenly I seemed to be clear, and fell forward on my face. I am not sure whether I fainted or not, but I must have lain there for some minutes. When I picked myself up I felt a light breeze upon my forehead and the mist was clearing away as quickly as it had come. I saw the rim of the moon above the horizon, and my mysterious fatigue had disappeared. I hurried forward as quickly as I could without venturing to look behind me. I only wanted to get out of that abominable drove on to the high-road, where there were lights and other human beings. For I knew that what I had seen was a creature of darkness and waste places, and that among my fellows I should be safe. When I reached home my housekeeper looked at me oddly. Of course my clothes were muddy and disarranged, but I suspect that there was something else unusual in my appearance. I merely said that I had had a fall coming up a drove in the dark, and was not feeling particularly well. I avoided the looking-glass when I went to my room to change.

Coming downstairs I heard through the open kitchen door some scraps of conversation--or rather of a monologue delivered by my housekeeper--to the effect that no one ought to be about the droves after dark as much as I was, and that it was a providence that things were no worse. Her own mother's uncle had--it appeared--been down just such another drove on just such another night, forty-two years ago come next Christmas Eve. 'They brought 'im 'ome on a barrow with both 'is eyes drawed down, and every drop of blood in 'is body turned. But 'e never would speak to what 'e see, and wild cats couldn't ha' scratched it out of him.'

An inaudible remark from one of the maids was met with a long sniff, and the statement: 'Girls seem to think they know everything nowadays.' I spent the next day in bed, as besides the shock which I had received I had caught a bad cold. When I got up on the second I was not surprised to hear that Mrs. Vries had been found dead on the previous afternoon. I had hardly finished breakfast when I was told that the policeman, whose name was Winter, would be glad to see me.

It appeared that on New Year's morning a half-witted boy of seventeen, who lived at one of the other cottages down the drove, had come to him and said that Mrs. Vries was dead, and that he must come and enter her house. He declined to explain how he had come by the information: so at first Mr. Winter contented himself with pointing out that it was the first of January not of April. But the boy was so insistent that finally he went. When repeated knockings at Mrs. Vries' cottage produced no result he had felt justified in forcing the back-door. She was sitting in a large wooden armchair quite dead. She was leaning forward a little and her hands were clasping the arms so tightly that it proved to be a matter of some difficulty to unloose her fingers. In front of her was another chair, so close that if anyone had been sitting in it his knees must have touched those of the dead woman. The seat cushions were flattened down as if it had been occupied recently by a solid personage. The tea-things had not been cleared away, but the kitchen was perfectly clean and tidy. There was no suspicion of foul play, as all the doors and windows were securely fastened on the inside. Winter added that her face made him feel 'quite sickish like,' and that the house smelt very bad for all that it was so clean.

A post-mortem examination of the body showed that her heart was in a very bad state, and enabled the coroner's jury to return a verdict of 'Death from Natural Causes.' But the doctor told me privately that she must have had a shock of some kind. ' In fact,' he said, if anyone ever died of fright, she did. But goodness knows what can have frightened her in her own kitchen unless it was her own conscience. But that is more in your line than mine.'

He added that he had found the examination of the body peculiarly trying: though he could not, or would not, say why.

As I was the last person who had seen her alive, I attended the inquest, but gave only formal evidence of an unimportant character. I did not mention that the second armchair had stood in a corner of the room during my visit, and that I had not occupied it.

The boy was of course called and asked how he knew she was dead. But nothing satisfactory could be got from him. He said that there was right houses and there was wrong houses--not to say persons--and that 'they 'had been after her for a long time. When asked whom he meant by 'they' he declined to explain, merely adding as a general statement that he could see further into a milestone than what some people could, for all they thought themselves so clever. His own family deposed that he had been absolutely silent, contrary to his usual custom, from tea-time on New Year's Eve to breakfast-time next day. Then he had suddenly announced that Mrs. Vries was dead; and ran out of the house before they could say anything to him. Accordingly he was dismissed, with a warning to the effect that persons who were disrespectful to Constituted Authorities always came to a bad end.

It naturally fell to me to conduct the funeral, as I could have given no reason for refusing her Christian burial. The coffin was not particularly weighty, but as it was being lowered into the grave the ropes supporting it parted, and it fell several feet with a thud. The shock dislodged a quantity of soil from the sides of the cavity, so that the coffin was completely covered before I had had time to say 'Earth to earth: Ashes to ashes: Dust to dust.'

Afterwards the sexton spoke to me apologetically about the occurrence. 'I'm fair put about, Sir, about them ropes,' he said. 'Nothing o' that sort ever 'appened afore in my time. They was pretty nigh new too, and I thought they'd a done us for years. But just look 'ere, Sir.' Here he showed two extraordinarily ravelled ends. 'I never see a rope part like that afore. Almost looks as if it 'ad been scratted through by a big cat or somethink.'

That night I was taken ill. When I was better my doctor said that rest and change of scene were imperative. I knew that I could never go down a drove alone by night again, so tendered my resignation to my Bishop. I hope that I have still a few years of usefulness before me: but I know that I can never be as if I had not seen what I have seen. Whether I met with my adventure through any fault of my own I cannot tell. But of one thing I am sure. There are powers of darkness which walk abroad in waste places: and that man is happy who has never had to face them.

If anyone who reads this should ever have a similar experience and should feel tempted to try to investigate it further, I commend to him the counsel of Jesus-ben-Sira.

My son, seek not things that are too hard for thee: and search not out things that are above thy strength.'

THE BLANK LEAVES

Mr. Edward Withington was a gentleman somewhat past middle-age. Deafness had compelled him to give up a considerable practice at the Bar, which his friends hoped would have raised him to the Bench. He was a widower without children, so his existence had become rather solitary.

Fortunately, however, he developed a strong taste for research into pedigrees and family history of all kinds. This led him to make numerous journeys to various parts of the country to make extracts from Parish Registers, copy tombstones and take rubbings of brasses; and so provided him with exactly the sort of occupation and interest which he needed.

It would be difficult to picture a much more placid pursuit. Indeed, to many people it might appear to be almost dull. But one of these expeditions led to a very curious experience, the history of which is here set down in his own words. He told it to me about three years after it had happened.

I was tracing the history of a family named Bolsover which I knew to have settled in Lincolnshire some time in the reign of Queen Elizabeth. And I had reason to believe that if I went to a little village, which I will call Snettersby, I should stand a good chance of gathering some of the information which I required.

Accordingly upon a fine afternoon towards the end of October I deposited myself at Scopperland, the nearest railway station, and having engaged a room at the inn for the night began to make some preliminary enquiries. I learned that Snettersby was about three miles off and that it possessed an inn which my landlord did not feel able to recommend. Having ascertained this much I thought I would walk over and have a look at it for myself. Unless the inn were quite impossible it would certainly be more convenient to be actually upon the spot, as otherwise I should have to waste a good deal of time in getting to and fro. (There were no motors in those days.)

My first impressions of Snettersby were favourable. It lay picturesquely enough round a village green--as is common in that part of England. Many of the cottages were of wood, but some were of old red brick which had mellowed to a very attractive tint. The church lay at one end, so screened with trees that only the top of the low square tower could be seen. The Rectory lay upon the far side of the churchyard and was not visible from the high-road. An early tea at *The Running Man* assured me that I should do well enough there for a day or two. So I engaged a bedroom for the following night and arranged to have my bag sent for in the morning.

On my arrival next day I went to the Rectory and explained the object of my visit. The Rector made no difficulty about letting me have the keys of the church and of the safe in the vestry where the parish registers were kept.

I did not spend much time in the church. It was a good-sized Perpendicular building dating from about 1440, to which some seventeenth-century additions had been made. It did not differ from scores of others. The painted glass I judged to have been put in about 1850. The artist had held that Biblical characters are best represented in yellow or magenta under-garments with cloaks of apple-green. As it was a bright sunny morning the effect was inexpressibly vivid. There were no interesting monuments; and as soon as I had made sure that the mural tablets contained nothing which I wanted I turned to the safe.

Now those who occupy their business in parochial registers know that they can never foretell their luck. Sometimes the books have been well kept and are in good condition. Sometimes, on the other hand, there are serious gaps in the entries or page after page has become illegible from damp. Sometimes an entire volume may be missing. But the Snettersby registers seemed to be as good as any which I have ever come across. The series was complete from 1558, the books had been carefully kept and were in perfect condition. To add to my satisfaction I picked up the Bolsovers almost immediately.

I was at work on the Register of Burials and had got past the middle of the seventeenth century when I came upon a page which differed from the rest. The entries did not cover more than two-thirds of it and the remaining space was filled with a number of meaningless marks. Or at any rate of marks which meant nothing to me. Some I recognized as Hebrew letters: one was undoubtedly a Greek *Phi*. Others suggested Runes, but I was not sufficiently familiar with Runic lettering to be sure. There were also a number of other marks which I thought stood for the signs of the Zodiac or something of that kind.

In all there were forty-five characters: nine in the top row, eight in the second and so on. The lines were all exactly the same distance apart and the characters in each were carefully spaced. Whatever the purpose of the performance might have been, considerable pains must have been expended on it.

'Well,' I thought, 'someone must have wasted some of his time over this. But as it can't help to fix the dates of the deaths of Tobias and Shelumiel Bolsover, which is what I am after at this moment, I don't see why it should lead me to waste any of mine.'

I turned over but found the next two pages blank. Probably they had stuck together when the book was new and so had been turned over as one by accident. On the third page the entries began again in a different hand.

At this point I thought it time to return to The Running Man for lunch. I left the book open upon the table with the written sheets containing the extracts which I had made beside it.

When I came back I noticed at once that my papers had been disarranged. I had left them in a neat heap with a sheet half-covered with writing on top. Now they were strewn all over the table and one or two were on the floor. A blank sheet lay beside the open volume as if inviting me to begin upon it.

My first thought was naturally that it had been done by a gust of wind. But the vestry window was shut, as it had been all the morning. I had locked the doors leading into the church and churchyard when I left and had taken the keys with me. But of course the clerk, or whoever was employed to clean the church, would be likely to have a duplicate set. He or she must have come in while I was away and disarranged my papers by accident.

I soon had them in order again and went on with my pursuit of the Bolsovers. I had found out all I wanted to know, and was just preparing to put away, as the light was beginning to fail, when it struck me that I might as well take a copy of the curious cypher or cryptogram--whichever is the proper name for it. I had a friend at Cambridge who was keenly interested in such things and would be likely to be able to tell me what, if anything, it meant.

I had brought some sheets of tracing-paper, so the copy was quickly made. I was just preparing to shut the book when a voice said very distinctly in my ear: *You ought to copy the blank leaves too.*'

It was low, but of the metallic timbre which even a deaf man can hear. Naturally I jumped. My first idea was of course that someone had come in unheard, as they might easily have done, and I looked round. But there was no one there. I don't think I had really expected that there would be.

I told myself that it was merely imagination, and prepared for the second time to close the book. But as I took it up the voice came again: *You must copy the blank leaves too.*'

Curiously I was not frightened. Of course I had been startled at first, but now I felt quite anxious to carry out my invisible friend's suggestion. But at this point a practical difficulty arose. The leaves undoubtedly were blank. So how could I or anybody else take a copy of them?

After a little consideration I hit upon what I thought a very ingenious device. I laid the book upon the table and spread a sheet of tracing-paper across it. On this I rested my hand with a pencil held lightly between my fingers, shut my eyes and waited.

I did not have to wait long. In a few seconds the pencil began to twitch, much as if someone had taken hold of the end. After a few feeble scratchings it began to travel rapidly over the paper, and I let my hand follow it. It went right round the sheet in a decided if irregular fashion and then stopped.

When I opened my eyes I had no difficulty in recognizing a ground plan of the church. At one point, just outside the north wall, there was a dot where the point of the pencil had nearly gone through the paper.

So far so good. The experiment had proved more interesting than I had expected. But there was still another leaf to be dealt with. So I took a second sheet of tracing-paper and arranged myself as before.

This time I did not have to wait at all. The pencil wrote something very rapidly and then snapped between my fingers. I opened my eyes and read the following verse from Isaiah. *Their houses shall be full of doleful creatures and owls shall dwell there and satyrs shall dance there.*

The hand was not my own. It was unquestionably identical with one of those in the register: namely, the one which came to an end at the blank leaves.

This, I must admit, disquieted me considerably. For it suggested that I had somehow put myself en rapport with some person unknown who might presently force a much closer acquaintance upon me. Still, the mischief, if any, was done now. I collected my papers, put away the book, locked up everything very carefully and returned the keys to the Rectory.

It was dark by the time I turned out of the Rectory gate, and though I had only a few hundred yards to walk to my inn I was glad when I got there. For on the way I was much annoyed by what seemed to be an unusually large bat, which kept flitting round my head, almost brushing my face with its wings. My efforts to drive it off were not successful, and though I was pretty sure that bats do not eat cats I did not feel certain that one so audacious as this might not scratch the face or bite the ears of a human being. When I got near the door of the inn it made off, and if I had trusted to appearances I could have sworn that it flitted straight into the house.

But this seemed so unlikely that I felt sure that my eyes must have been deceived.

Between tea and supper I occupied myself with going over my notes on the Bolsover family to make sure that I had got them complete. This done, my thoughts naturally turned to the cryptogram and my copy of the blank leaves. But I could make nothing of either. Then I must, I suppose, have fallen asleep. I say 'I suppose' because I can only ascribe my subsequent experience to a dream, though it was at the time, and still remains, as vivid as anything which ever befell me in my waking moments.

First the inn-parlour in which I was sitting seemed to elongate itself until I found myself gazing down a vista of great length. At the far end there was considerable activity of some sort, but I could not discern exactly what was taking place. There appeared to be a number of people gathered round a raised platform of some kind. On this a solitary figure presently appeared. Before I could make out more the whole scene had vanished.

I stared at the darkness for a minute or two. Then a point of light appeared, as if at the end of a long tunnel. It advanced slowly, and there could be no doubt that it was a lamp of some kind which some person unknown was carrying. As it got nearer I felt that there was something curious and uncanny about it, though I could not have said exactly what. But I felt very unwilling to see it or its bearer at close quarters. I tried hard to make him out, but could see nothing of him at all. Before long this too disappeared and there was nothing but darkness.

I was sitting beside a fire and had two candles on the table beside me. But naturally their light did not extend very far. Beyond it the blackness was impenetrable and gave me a sensation of infinite distance.

Presently I became aware--I say advisedly became 'aware,' because I did not see or hear anything--that the room was full of stealthy movement. Certainly there was somebody there and he seemed to be pacing softly to and fro, as you may see hungry tigers doing in their cages at the zoo.

Was he preparing for a spring?

Suddenly from the edge of the darkness what looked like an arm was protruded and very quickly withdrawn. I noticed that it was naked, black, and very thin. There was something else unpleasant about it which I did not take in at the moment. But on thinking it over afterwards I realized what it was. The arm had no hand. It ended in a stump at the wrist.

At this point the door burst open and the landlord tumbled into the room with a scared expression on his usually placid countenance.

'Beg pardon, Sir,' he said, 'but is anything the matter? Did you want anything?'

'No,' I replied. 'I didn't ring.'

'No, Sir--I know you didn't. There ain't no bell to begin with. But we thought we 'eard you call out three times, Sir--all on us did. Something 'orrible it sounded, in a manner of speaking, if you'll excuse me saying of it.'

I told him that I had fallen asleep in front of the fire and must have cried out in my sleep. I apologized for the fright I had given to the household and he withdrew apparently reassured.

But I did not believe that I had been asleep, and was quite sure that whoever had called out it was not I.

Happening to look up at the ceiling some play of firelight cast a shadow like the form of a very large bat. But it was only a shadow and disappeared immediately.

The appearance of the room was now entirely normal and the rest of the evening passed uneventfully. So did the night, and by the afternoon of the next day I was back in London.

The next part of the story begins with two letters which Mr. Withington received some six weeks after his visit to Snettersby. They explain themselves so I subjoin them in full:

Sandford College, Cambridge.
Dec. 15th, 1912.

Dear Withington,

Many thanks for the cryptogram. It's a curious thing and I never saw one quite like it before. Of the forty-five characters, twelve are the zodiacal signs and seven the planetary symbols. The remaining twenty-six are letters. You were right in thinking that eleven of them are Runes. There is one Greek, and the other fourteen are Hebrew.

I thought that the presence of a solitary Greek letter meant that Greek was the language. I transliterated accordingly and after a little juggling got the following sentence:

(greek characters displayed in here in the printed book)

(Let us stand in righteousness, let us stand in fear.)

The phrase comes in the Greek liturgies and had a great vogue in the west as a charm. I don't suppose most of the people who used it knew what it meant or where it came from.

I don't doubt that is what it is here. It looks as if your friend had dabbled a bit in unlawful arts. But what precisely he thought he was up to I can't say.

Yours ever, J. L. Masters. * * *

The Rectory,
Snettersby,
Lincolnshire.

Dec. 16th, 1912.

Dear Sir,

I must ask you to forgive me for what may seem to be an impertinent enquiry. But I hope you will recognize that I have good grounds for making it.

When you examined our Registers in October did you notice anything remarkable in them, or did anything in any way odd or unusual befall you? I ask because ever since your visit our quiet village has been troubled in a curious and quite inexplicable manner. The disturbances, which it seems difficult to assign to any natural cause, have increased steadily until life has become almost intolerable.

On the day of your departure a labourer who happened to be passing the churchyard after dark was pelted with stones and clods of earth. After this had happened several times to other people we set a watch--assuming naturally that it was the doing of some mischievous boy. But we could find no one, and our vigilance seemed only to increase the activity of our invisible assailant. On other occasions people have been thrown violently to the ground without being able to see who had attacked them.

Beside this we have been visited by a perfect plague of owls and bats. The hooting of the owls makes sleep difficult at night, and the bats find their way into the houses in a most extraordinary fashion.

Nothing has as yet occurred during the daytime. But with the approach of dark the entire village falls into a state of panic which is evidently shared by the animals. The horses seem to feel it most and in two or three cases have become quite unmanageable.

So far no serious injury has been inflicted upon anyone: but we cannot tell what the next development may be. As the beginning of the disturbances seems to have coincided with your visit I am writing to you in the hope--I admit a faint one--that you may be able to throw some light upon them.

Yours very faithfully,
James R. Towers.

Two hours after the receipt of these letters Mr. Withington was in the train on his way to Cambridge. A long consultation with Masters resulted in the despatch of a telegram asking whether they could both be put up at the Rectory for a day or two. The following afternoon found them at Snettersby, and from this point the story can be most conveniently continued in Mr. Withington's own words.

By the time we had finished what we had to tell it was dark, and I think we were all conscious that a slightly creepy feeling had come over us. This was evidently shared by an Airedale who was lying stretched upon the hearth-rug. He made two or three uneasy movements and sniffed the air in a very suspicious fashion. Suddenly he jumped up and ran across the room to the right-hand window--we were in the study, a long room on the ground floor with three windows giving on to the garden. He then gave several short but furious barks, turned tail and went back to his place upon the rug.

Immediately afterwards we heard a drumming sound upon the pane. For a moment we thought it might have been made by a bird's wing. But it was too regular for that. We stole across the room and drew back the curtains. The sound was now more distinct, though considerably muffled by the shutters. It was such as might be made by the palm of a human hand beating steadily against the glass. It reminded me of an episode in *The House by the Churchyard*, by Joseph Sheridan Le Fanu, and I did not like it any the better for that. It certainly suggested that there was someone outside particularly anxious to attract our attention: or possibly to make his way into the house.

We were not at all sure that we were anxious for his company, but after a moment's hesitation we unbarred the shutters. As we did so the sound ceased. Directly afterwards it began at the middle window. But as soon as the shutters were opened it transferred itself to the left-hand end. Pursued there it returned to the middle. We could see nothing, but did not like to open a window for fear of what we might admit. When we separated and each stood at a window the sound ceased altogether. But as soon as a window was left deserted it began again.

None of us liked it at all. But as we had come to Snettersby to see the thing through we felt bound to take a bold line. So Masters and I decided to go round outside while the Rector stayed in the room to observe what he could. The Airedale absolutely declined to accompany us.

It was a dark night, cloudy, with no moon. The door was not upon the same side of the house as the study windows, so we had a corner to turn. We crept round it cautiously. I was armed with an electric torch but had not turned it on for fear of scaring our visitor prematurely.

When we were round the corner we saw the three broad belts of light coming from the three windows. Mr. Towers was standing at the middle one and his shadow made a dark smudge upon the grass. There was nothing else to be seen and nothing to be heard.

Then as we looked the shadow began to change its shape--though we could see that Mr. Towers had not moved. It contracted to an irregular blotch like a person--or was it an animal?--crouching upon the ground. Then it began to oscillate backwards and forwards--as if preparing for a spring. Then a dark arm or feeler shot out from it and was pressed against the glass. I turned on my torch and as I did so the whole thing disappeared, exactly as a real shadow would have done. There was absolutely nothing there.

When we returned to the house Mr. Towers had not much to add to our story. As soon as we had left the room the drumming ceased. He had remained standing at the window to keep a look-out for anything unusual. But there was nothing to be seen except his own shadow upon the grass. Then he saw as we had done that it was changing its shape. It contracted and thickened until he could make out the form of a person wrapped in a dark cloak of some sort crouching upon the grass. A head protruded, perfectly bald and lolling horribly as if the neck were broken. Then an arm shot out and was pressed against the glass. It had no hand but ended in a black spongy mass which was squeezed against the pane. The effect of this was so indescribably disgusting that it made him feel inclined to be sick.

Then the light of my torch fell upon the creature, and there was nothing there.

We divided the night into watches. Two of us sat up together while the third slept. But nothing unusual occurred.

Next morning we decided that the only thing which could be done was to go to the church to see whether any explanation of our experiences could be found there. We felt pretty sure that nothing further could happen in the daytime.

Naturally we began with the Register of Burials. But when we turned to the place from which I had copied the charm it was no longer there. The entries only covered two-thirds of the page as before. But the remaining third was blank. The Rector was positive that no one had touched the volume since I had had it, as he always kept the keys of the safe himself. And Masters' expert eye could detect no trace of any erasure.

On turning over we had surprise number two. The next two pages were no longer blank as I had seen them, but were filled with entries of the usual kind. There was nothing surprising about the sequence of dates. The last before the place from which I had copied the charm was 21 July, 1672: the first after it, in a different hand which continued for several years, was 14 October of the same year.

Our only remaining hope seemed to be in my plan of the church and we could think of no better course than to dig at the point outside the north wall where my pencil had made a deep dot in the paper. If this should involve the illegality of opening a grave that could not be helped. Fortunately the place was upon the side of the church away from the village. The churchyard was not a thoroughfare and was well screened by trees. So we were pretty safe from interruption.

We got three spades from the Rector's potting-shed and set to work. Being amateurs our progress was rather slow and it was not until we had got down about three feet that I struck my spade upon something hard. This proved to be a small object some ten inches square by five deep. It was thickly coated with pitch and as it was not heavy we judged it to be a wooden box.

Here at any rate was a find. We took it to the Rectory and got tools to break it open. This took some little time as we had to chip the pitch off with a chisel before we could find the fastening of the lid. But at last we came upon some screws, which proved easier to turn than we had expected.

The box contained a small and very light package done up in canvas. We unripped this carefully and Masters unrolled it upon the table. We found a dried human hand: a right hand which had been severed at the wrist with a very sharp instrument. The skin was intact but there seemed to be no vestige of fat or gristle between it and the bones. The finger-tips were blackened as if they had been scorched by fire.

Of course this made us certain that we were on the right track. But as there were still a good many gaps to be filled in we turned again to the box to see whether it had any more information for us. Sticking to the bottom was a small wad of paper tightly folded. It was not easy to detach this without tearing it. But at last we got it off in good condition. The inside contained some lines of writing and though the ink was a good deal faded, Masters, who was very expert in such matters, had little difficulty in deciphering it. It was in a late seventeenth-century hand and ran as follows--

'Ye hande of Richd. Partridge sometyme Clerke of this Parysshe who was hanged upon September ye Firste in ye yeare of oure Lord 1672. I have done worse and suffer ye rewarde of my misdedes. Lord, have mercy upon me. WM. ARCHER.'

'H'm,' I said, 'there's evidently a history here. I wonder what it is? And we seem to be nearly as far as ever from any satisfactory explanation. I suppose it was Partridge who came to the house last night. Are we to offer him his hand if he comes again, or what?'

For the last few minutes Masters had been looking very grave. He now said suddenly and with great emphasis--Burn those tracings of yours. I don't think I'm a superstitious man. But I don't like this one little bit. And so I say burn them.'

We were standing in front of the fire in the study. I took the three sheets from my pocket and without saying anything further threw them on to the blaze. I had been intimate with Masters for many years, and knew that he was not easily moved, and did not say what he did not mean.

They caught at once; a feather of ash whirled up the chimney and was gone.

'Well,' I said, 'that's the end of them. But now what are we to do with the hand?'

We turned to look at it, where we had left it lying upon the table--but it was gone. The box was there, and the canvas wrapper; so was the paper. But of the hand itself there was not the slightest trace. Yet we had not had our backs turned for more than a few seconds. While we stared blankly at one another there came from somewhere outside the melancholy hoot of an owl.

'There are two things I want to do now,' said Masters, 'and if you'll both come with me we can just manage them before the light goes. First, I want to put back the box where it came from, and then I want to have another look at the Register.'

The first task was quickly performed. We had cut the top sods carefully, and when we had put them back felt satisfied that in a few weeks the place would show very few signs of having been disturbed.

Then we adjourned to the vestry. Masters, who had remained silent since we left the house, took the seventeenth-century volume and began to read the entries: while we waited. He had hardly had the book in his hands for more than a minute when he said, half to himself and half to us--'I thought as much.' Then he read aloud 'September 5th, 1673, William Archer. Dyed September 1st. The verdict of the Crowner's Quest was The Visitation of God.'

'Visitation of God,' he went on. Wm. I fancy we are in a position to correct that verdict. Partridge must have got him all right, on the anniversary of his own execution too! I wonder how he managed it? That's all. Let's go back.'

At a later hour in the evening he consented to give us his theory of what had occurred.

'I have never been able,' he said, to dismiss witchcraft, etcetera, as lightly as some people do. I don't profess to be able to explain it. Perhaps there isn't any explanation. Or perhaps it is really too simple to need one. But anyhow I think it is a force which has to be reckoned with. More perhaps in the past than to-day. But it isn't dead yet. Partridge must have been up to devilry of some kind--it would be interesting to know whether he was hanged for that or for something commonplace like murder or highway robbery--and he meant something by that charm. He seems to have had a pretty apt pupil in Mr. Archer too.

Did you ever hear of The Hand of Glory? It comes in one of the Ingoldsby Legends, you know. If you could get the right hand of a corpse and turn it into a lamp by fixing a wick steeped in *human* fat to each finger-tip the highest walks of burglary were open to you at once. On the approach of the hand everyone falls into a sleep from which no noise can wake them, and all locks and bolts fly open of their own accord. If the original proprietor of the hand does happen to have been hanged--so much the better. Well--no doubt that was Archer's game--or one of his games.

Partridge didn't like it, for which I don't blame him myself: and I expect he gave Archer a pretty bad time. Archer got frightened, and as he couldn't get at Partridge's body again for some reason did the best he could by burying the hand.

Well--Partridge got him all right as we know. But he still wanted his hand and didn't know how to come at that. I expect the fact that it was in consecrated ground was what defeated him. When you started digging in his volume of the Registers, which probably hadn't been touched for a couple of centuries--I noticed that the last entry was 1703--he thought he saw a chance. And when you copied his charm you, as it were, wound the machine up and he could get to work. He gave you a clue and a warning--both rather vague I admit--and followed that up with his show at the inn. When you left Snettersby he had got to get you back somehow--and he succeeded at last. Well, he's got his hand now, and I hope he finds it useful wherever he is.'

Here Masters paused for a moment to attend to his whisky-and-soda. When this had been dealt with satisfactorily he went on--

'Of course there are several gaps in the story which we can't fill in. I don't know why Partridge, since he could tell you to copy the blank leaves, couldn't go about the rest of the job more directly. All that can be said is that gentlemen of his condition always do adopt what seem to us to be very roundabout methods. Whether that is due to choice or circumstances, I don't know. But I suspect the latter. In fact their ways--as the Irish orator observed of those of Providence--are indeed unscrupulous! However, I think we are rid of him now.'

A few months later I heard from Mr. Towers that there had been no further disturbances of any kind. He expressed a hope that I would come and pay him a visit. But I have never gone to Snettersby again and as I have learned all I wanted to know about the Bolsover family I don't suppose I ever shall.

THE THIRTEENTH TREE

If, as I incline to think, architecture in general and domestic architecture in particular is the best expression of the characteristics of the period to which it belongs, there would be a good deal to be said in favour of having been born soon after the year 1570.

Late Tudor or early Jacobean houses always seem to me to exhibit the qualities which I admire most. They are dignified and beautiful without conscious effort. Both inside and out I find them extraordinarily satisfying. 'This,' I say to myself, 'is what a country-house ought to be.' They look as if they had grown from the soil as naturally as the trees in their parks. They are as they are because the men who planned them were solid, dignified and sure of themselves.

Castles speak of violence and cruelty, until they have become an anachronism. Then they are sights to be seen rather than houses to live in. Early Tudor houses have something upstart about them; as, it may be suspected, had their owners. The Palladian palaces of the eighteenth century are not free from ostentation. They were meant to display the wealth and taste of their owners, most of whom had probably made the Grand Tour. Despite their dignity and internal comfort I can never feel that they belong to the English countryside. But the type of house which was built about twenty years on either side of the year 1600 always seems to me to escape all these defects. One of them was the scene of the story which I am now going to tell.

It is situated in one of the western counties. That is as much as I shall say about its geographical position, as I do not want to bring the *Society for Spectral Investigations*, or any similar body, about my ears or those of the neighbourhood.

I had known the owner when we were boys. Our paths in life had diverged and for thirty years or more we never met. We came across each other accidentally in London, and both welcomed the opportunity of resuming an old friendship. When he asked me to visit him I was very glad to accept his invitation. Accordingly, a few weeks later, on a fine day early in October, I caught a train at Paddington for my journey westwards.

I had made acquaintance with the first twenty miles of the Great Western in the year 1890, and for some time after that they had been very familiar to me. But I had not travelled by that route for a good many years and was horrified to see how the Great Wen (as Cobbett rudely called London) had spread over what I remembered as pleasant countryside. One of the few things which did not seem to have altered since I had passed that way last was a building of really exceptional ugliness (a hotel, I believe) close to the station at Slough. For, I think, the first time in my life the sight of it gave me real pleasure.

I had to change three times in the course of my journey and it was nearly five o'clock when I got out at the country station where my host met me. The light was failing when we arrived at the house and I could only see that it was large, and that it promised to be very beautiful.

I was introduced to my hostess and her two daughters, and after tea in the hall in front of a superb log-fire in a large open fireplace my host took me to the smoking-room.

'I had no idea you were such a territorial magnate,' I said to him when we had settled down.

'I never expected to be,' he said. My father was a parson in the north, and I became a solicitor in York--as you know. We lived just outside York for the first fifteen years after I was married. I knew of this place, but never saw it until I succeeded a distant cousin (whom I never saw either) nearly seven years ago. He was unmarried and a queer-tempered old chap by all accounts. Perhaps the fact that he had never seen me influenced his choice of an heir. The place isn't entailed and there were several distant relations beside me. It's a curious thing, but this property has never passed in the direct male line since Sir Robert Newton, whose portrait you'll see in the dining-room, bought it and built the house, about the year 1602 I believe. He was Chief Justice of the Queen's Bench. His son was drowned in a pool in the garden. It does not exist now. It was filled in immediately afterwards. No one could ever understand how the boy got into it, or why, having got in, he couldn't get out, as it was quite shallow I believe, and he was more than a child. There was a daughter who married and brought her family here after her parents' death. But her son was killed at Naseby, leaving several daughters. And so it has gone on. Either there has been no son or he hasn't lived to inherit. My immediate predecessor succeeded a childless uncle, and as we have only two daughters we keep up the tradition. I'm really almost glad I never had a son, as I am sure my wife would be nervous about bringing him here. Indeed, I don't mind admitting that I think I should be. Of course the village people say there's a curse on the place, but they don't know why. I can't think that my respected ancestor--he is my ancestor, if by no means in the direct line--was likely to have done anything to provoke one.'

Certainly when I looked at the portrait an hour or two later I could detect nothing evil in it. It suggested that Sir Robert had been a shrewd and kindly person, who would probably be as lenient on the Bench as the law allowed him to be. No doubt he had passed many sentences in his time which we should think harsh or even savage. But that would not have been the view of his contemporaries.

After dinner we sat in the library. It was a large room completely lined with well-filled bookcases whose contents looked as if they would repay examination. There is no saying what may not have wandered into such a place; just as any oyster may contain a pearl of price. I asked whether there was a catalogue.

'Not a very good one,' was the answer. 'In fact I'm not sure that I shan't spend a good part of this winter trying to improve it. You'd like to have a look round it tomorrow, I expect. A good many of the books belonged to Sir Robert. By the way, we've put you in what is said to have been his bedroom. It isn't often used, but we've just had to take up the floors in some of the rooms nearer ours; dry rot, pretty bad too. But I think you'll be quite comfortable there. No; there's no story about it that I ever heard. We don't run to a ghost of any kind.'

We went upstairs soon afterwards, and while I was undressing I meditated upon the queer fatality which seemed to have pursued the family for three hundred years. Was it more than a series of odd and unfortunate coincidences? Are there, or have there ever been, people who had some malign power which they could direct against their enemies? If it were so, how was this power operative after their lifetime? Did it exhaust itself after a period of time or not?

I had finished undressing before I had arrived at a satisfactory answer to any of these conundrums. When I was ready for bed I went to the window, opened it and drew back the curtains as was my custom. It was a clear night with a good deal of moon. My room was on the first floor at the back of the house, overlooking a part of the garden which I had not seen before. Immediately below me lay a gravelled terrace, bounded on the far side by a stone balustrade. On the other side of this, at a lower level and reached by a flight of steps, lay a small formal garden. In the middle was a circular stone basin, where I hoped there might be a fountain. Round the edge stood a number of dark clipped trees--yews or cypresses I could not tell which. There were twelve of these: one at each corner and two in between. On the far side was a low stone wall separating the garden from the park beyond. Very white it looked in the moonlight; almost as if it were newly built. About the middle there was a dark patch; ivy or creeper I supposed. It made a clump on the coping and then spread sideways, in a way which almost suggested the head and arms of a person in the act of climbing the wall. I thought it rather ugly and decided that if I were the owner I would have it removed. Then I went to bed.

For some reason sleep did not come as quickly as usual and I was visited with the pictures--half-dreams and halfwaking--which belong to the border-line of consciousness. Mine made two scenes. In the first I found myself seated in a large old-fashioned travelling coach. Beside me was a figure very much wrapped up. He turned towards me once as if about to speak, and I recognized the original of the portrait in the dining-room. Presently we were brought to a standstill by a great concourse of people who seemed to be streaming away from some spectacle. I put my head out of the window to see what it was, but drew it in again quickly. A few yards in front of us was a gallows and there were four bodies dangling from the cross-beam. As I sat down, feeling as if I should be sick, a head was poked in at the window on the other side. It belonged to a young man. The face seemed unnaturally pale. There was something else unusual about it, but I could not take in what it was. The young man said something in a low tone to my companion. I could not catch the words, but they seemed to disconcert him very much. Next moment the face had vanished and we had begun to move again. I woke fully to find myself murmuring, *An eye for an eye and a tooth for a tooth.*'

The second scene was a churchyard by night. A funeral was taking place. I could see the bearers and the men with the torches and the priest. But there appeared to be no mourners, unless I were one. As the coffin was lowered into the grave some bird of the night gave a long and dolorous screech very close overhead. At this I woke. I think there must have been a hunting owl or a night-jar outside my window. As I did not wish for any repetition of such scenes I got a book and read until I could feel confident that I should sleep soundly.

When I went to my window next morning I received a surprise. There, as was to be expected, was the garden on which I had looked the night before. But there were no trees and no pool, and I could see no growth upon the wall at the bottom. Yet I *knew* that I had seen those things, and that I had not been dreaming at the time. I decided to say nothing about them. When we went out after breakfast, however, I did ask my host whether he knew where the pool in which Sir Robert's son had been drowned had been. But he did not. I noticed that the wall between the garden and park did not look as new as I had thought it the night before. It seemed to be the same age as the rest of the house, as was to be expected. That might, however, be due to the difference between daylight and moonlight. The day was fine and as the neighbourhood was new to me, most of the hours of daylight were passed out-of-doors. After tea, when we were sitting in the library, I asked my host whether he knew why or by whom the curse had been laid upon Sir Robert's descendants.

'Well,' said he, 'there is a bit of a story about it. But all I know is very incomplete and doesn't explain much. It seems that in the old judge's time there was a woman in the village who was reputed to be a witch. Nothing very out of the way about that. In fact you wouldn't have to look very far to find witches (or reputed ones) in these west-country villages to-day. Her name was Miriam Urch (Urch is quite a common name in these parts) and they say that she was at the bottom of it. But I don't know why she should have had a down on the Newtons, and as nothing was ever proved against her she was given Christian burial in the churchyard when her time came. You can see what is said to be her grave close to the north door. I expect it is. Village tradition is generally pretty accurate on such points. They aren't quite sure whether she is always in it though, even now. I believe the Rector has had something to say to old Job Dixon the sexton about its untidiness more than once. But *he* says it isn't his fault. There are no other graves anywhere near it, and I don't think there will be as long as there is a scrap of room anywhere else.'

No more was said on the topic that evening and the hours after dinner passed pleasantly with a game of bridge with my host and his two daughters. We were all agreed that games are games, and though due respect must be paid to the rules which govern them they ought not to be transformed into hard and dismal forms of work.

It was near midnight before I found myself in my room, and when I was ready for bed I admit that I hesitated for a moment before drawing back my curtains. Finally curiosity prevailed. If there were anything to be seen I might as well see it. It seemed unlikely that any harm could come to me, or to the family through me.

I looked out. The moon shone brilliantly, and there, beyond any possibility of mistake, were the pool and the twelve trees. But were there only twelve? My first impression was that there were more. That was absurd. I counted them again just to make sure, and, as I had thought, there was one at each corner with two in between. But as soon as I looked at them all together I got the impression that there were more. But I could not have said where the additional one (I felt sure it was only one) was, nor even whether it were always in the same place. And I noticed that the ivy, or whatever it had been on the wall at the bottom, was gone. It might have been cleared away during the day, but I had an uncomfortable feeling that someone or something had come over and was dodging about behind the trees. If so, with what intent?

I began to feel an overpowering desire to go and investigate. Yet I could hardly do that. The door leading to the terrace was doubtless locked and bolted, and I should be sure to disturb someone in getting it open. What could I say if I did? That I thought it a fine night for a stroll and that I always found pyjamas the most comfortable wear for a nocturnal ramble? For I felt quite certain--I don't know why--that the trees and pool would be invisible to anyone except myself. All the same, the desire to investigate more closely grew stronger and stronger. I have never seen or experienced hypnotism, but began to feel as I imagine a hypnotic subject does. It seemed as if I was being dragged out by some force which was overpowering my own will, and that if I could not get the door open I should have to jump from my first-floor window. This would never do. As an antidote I began to recite the first thing which came into my head. It happened to be the *Battle of Lake Regillus* from Macaulay's *Days of Ancient Rome* and not for the first time I blessed the wisdom of my mother who had made us all learn quantities of poetry by heart as soon as we could read. This particular poem had been my first major achievement in this line. It had always remained particularly distinct in my memory because the recitation of it had won two new half-crowns from a godfather*, and thereby had enabled me to understand (for the first and last time in my life) what is meant by 'the possession of wealth beyond the dreams of avarice.'

[* He subsequently became Chief Justice of Trinidad, and was long remembered for his patience with garrulous witnesses, and the fervid eloquence of coloured advocates.]

I am not quite sure whether I declaimed it aloud or not. But I know that I had only got to the end of the first stanza:

But the proud Ides when the squadron rides
Shall be Rome's whitest day

when the spell, which I was quite sure had been malevolent, broke and I was completely my own master again. I felt as one does when a motor-car or bicycle has skidded and disaster in a ditch has been escaped by inches. I stopped at the window because I felt sure that something was going to happen. I did not have to wait long. A figure appeared on the terrace; where it had come from I did not see. When it emerged from the shadow of the house I saw that it was that of a young man; not much more than a boy. He seemed to be dressed as a young gentleman of quality would have been about the year 1600 or a little later. For some reason this did not surprise me. I wondered whether I was spying upon a lovers' meeting. The moonlight was all that could be desired, if the air were a little chilly. But there was no second figure to be seen. He went down the stone steps leading from the terrace to the garden below and advanced to the edge of the pool. He stood there for a minute or two looking down into the water. Perhaps he was admiring the reflection of the moon. Then a very horrid thing happened. A vague black shape darted from behind one of the trees and flung itself upon him. It lay on top of him and had obviously forced him into the pool face downwards with intent to drown him. I tried to shout--though what good that could have done I don't know. But no sound would come. I thought of going to the rescue, but found myself unable to move. Of course that would have been equally futile could I have got there. The next minute a heavy bank of cloud which had been creeping up from the south-west drove across the moon and I could see no more. There was no sound to be heard. How long I remained looking out of the window into blackness and silence, I cannot say. Presently I found that I could move again, so crept into bed. There was nothing more which I could have done. I think I slept more than might have been expected.

Next morning when we went into the library after breakfast, I decided that I must make an effort and tell my host what I had seen. It did need an effort, for I felt very unwilling to speak about it. I don't know why. I don't think I was afraid of being laughed at and if I were told that I had been dreaming I could only reply that I knew that I had been awake. Somehow that made me the more reluctant. However, I took the plunge.

He listened to my story very attentively, and obviously took it seriously. When I had finished he said--'I think we know now how poor young Newton came by his end. But who do you suppose it was that fell upon him? Mrs. Urch? If so, why?'

Neither of us said anything more for a little while. I could see that, like Odysseus on more than one occasion, he was this way and that dividing his swift mind. Then he said, Yes. I think there's sufficient reason. Wait a bit.'

We were sitting beside the fireplace as the morning was chilly. He went to the other end of the room, climbed to the top of a short step-ladder and took a smallish tin box from the end of a shelf. I saw that it was tied up with string or tape and that there was a seal over the knot. There was a label attached on which was written, in what looked like an early eighteenth-century hand, *Sir Robert Newton. Secreta. Not to be opened without sufficient reason.*'

'Well?' I said.

'Well,' he replied. 'Don't you think there is now?' Of course I agreed and the string was cut.

The most important part of the contents was a notebook. The handwriting was Elizabethan, and brief inspection satisfied us that the book had belonged to the judge. It was not exactly a diary. By no means were all the entries dated, and there did not seem to have been any attempt to produce a complete record of the period covered, which amounted to several years. There were a number of rather cryptic notes, apparently relating to cases which he had tried. Whether these were meant to direct his summing up or were merely private memoranda was not easy to decide. Neither of us was an expert palaeographer, and to decipher them all would obviously take some time. So we put the book aside for the moment.

There were several letters from Lady Newton from which it was to be inferred that she had gone down to the west to supervise the completion and furnishing of the new house while her husband was detained by work in London. These told a not unfamiliar tale of dilatory workmen, of things ordered from a distance which were not delivered on the day appointed and so forth. She also feared that when all was done the original estimate would be very much exceeded. (It would have been very interesting had she mentioned the sums, but unfortunately she did not.) These belonged to the years 1599-1600. As one of them referred to the good effect produced by 'your visit' it would appear that the judge had made an excursion to the scene of action to see whether he could expedite matters and alleviate some of his wife's troubles.

Underneath these was a largish sheet of paper which had been folded more than once. This proved to be a plan of the house and gardens--obviously by a professional hand. You will not be surprised to hear that in the middle of the small garden below the terrace was a circle of considerable size, which obviously indicated a pool. At a distance of some yards were twelve dots at regular intervals forming a square, to show where it was intended to place statues or plant trees or something of the sort. The plan itself did not state what form of ornament the architect had in mind. But I was in a position to say Trees not Statues.

There was only one more paper. This was merely a list of about a hundred names, presumably those of the inhabitants of the village, who were all the judge's tenants. This was dated 7 May, 1603, which my host thought must have been very soon after Sir Robert had come to reside permanently in his new home. It suggested that he had begun to devote himself seriously to the duties of a country gentleman. The name of Miriam Urch appeared among them. It was marked with an X but there was no note relating to her to be found. She must have lived alone, as the names were obviously arranged according to their households and there were no other Urches in the village. Beyond establishing the trustworthiness of tradition--up to a point--this did not get us much farther. Still, it was something to know that, witch or not, she really had existed. And there did seem to have been some special point of contact, however small, between her and the judge.

At this moment lunch was announced, so our investigation was suspended.

When we felt disposed to resume our researches, I suggested that it might be worth while to ask the Rector for permission to examine the Register of Burials at the church; supposing it to be in existence. So much was destroyed wantonly during the Commonwealth period that it is not uncommon to find no records prior to 1662. Here, however, we were in luck. The registers were complete from 1558 onwards. 7 May, 1603, was our *terminus a quo* and we found the entry of the burial of Miriam Urch on 4 November in that year. She had died on 31 October. There was an asterisk in the margin and at the foot of the page (we thought in another hand but could not be sure)

Under Ye Yew tree by ye north doore.

This was the only note appended to any entry in the volume. It might be presumed that her estate was not sufficient to provide a head-stone for the grave and that no one else was prepared to bear the expense. Also that somebody, whether at the time or afterwards, was anxious that the site should not be forgotten.

We turned on. The entries were few as the population of the village was small. We found the burial of Philip Newton, aged 19 years, on 7 November, 1604. He had died three days before.

I said, 'coincidences do happen. But this seems a little too close not to have been arranged. We know, more or less, how it was done. But I wonder why. There must be a story of some kind behind it.'

Our only remaining source of information was the judge's notebook, so we returned to that. The next day was so wet that there was nothing to distract us and as we became familiar with his hand we found that we could read most of it without much difficulty. The impression which we had formed on our first cursory inspection was confirmed. There were a number of disconnected memoranda, relating to a variety of matters. Some were dated, but not all. They seemed to cover the last ten or twelve years of his term upon the Bench. Some were concerned with cases which he had heard; others with purely domestic matters. Some were too short to be fully intelligible. It looked as if it had been Sir Robert's practice to put down from time to time whatever happened to be passing through his mind (not necessarily every day) without attempting to keep a systematic diary. One of the longest entries was a very noble prayer (apparently his own composition) that he might be enabled to do justice 'in the fear of God and with no fear of man.' Shortly after this was another prayer for forgiveness for any failure. It was clear that he had been a conscientious judge and had set himself a high standard. Interesting as much of this was, it was not relevant to our immediate purpose. We had got to almost the last page before we came upon anything which threw any light on the subject of our investigation.

The last case which he heard before his retirement, or at any rate the last of which there was any record, was of four men for highway robbery committed on Hounslow Heath. Their names were given: Roger Hewitson, William Parrett, Edward Backhouse and George Urch. The first three were bracketed together with the words Taken red-handed written against them. But for some reason the case against George Urch seems to have been less clear. His name was followed by a few jottings:

Taken next day. No good alibi. Identified on oath.

Then followed two or three lines which were quite illegible. Below them the words *Condemned with the others.*

The only other entries were purely personal. After this trial, but at what interval it was impossible to say, both his health and his spirits seemed to have been affected. Twice he recorded *Kept my chamber all day.* Once he had sent for the apothecary (to whom he had paid two shillings and sixpence). Another entry showed that he had paid a visit to the rector of S. Margaret's, Westminster. This ended with the word *Comforted.* From which it would appear that whatever his trouble was, it was not entirely physical. At this time his .wife and family must have been elsewhere, as he spoke of arranging for his man (whose name was Edward Hilyar) to lie in the little chamber next to mine '--and more than once had E. H. to sit with me in the parlour.'

It is a reasonable guess that George Urch the highwayman was the son of Miriam Urch, and that it was within her knowledge that Sir Robert had sent him to his death. Whether justly or not would not perhaps have concerned her very closely. But the judge's own jottings suggested that there might have been a miscarriage of justice; involuntary on his part. She seems to have had her revenge; if, in the strict sense of the word, she did not live to see it.

We returned to the churchyard. What tradition called her grave could be identified without difficulty as there were no others near it. But there was no vestige of any yew tree. There was, however, a shallow depression, roughly circular and of considerable extent close to it. We had recourse to the Rector again, not without apologies. He was able to tell us that he believed that there had been a tree there and that there were one or two old people living in the place who might remember something about it. He promised to ascertain what he could and added that, while he did not wish to appear discourteous, he thought he would be more likely to be successful if he pursued his investigations alone.

He had some information for us next day. There had been a yew tree there, which had been blown down in a terrible storm not long after Victoria became queen. 'It were more than two-under year old, but it were a good riddance.' (No explanation of this was forthcoming.)

'Wold rector had roots grubbed and tooken away and burned. When the men got under there was a gurt twod settin', and he spit at they zo dellish (query devilishly) that they were frit and run for rector. When they come back he were gone. Never zaw he no more. Rector came back wi' 'em and some things were found; bits o' bone and suchlike. Rector he wrapped up they and took they away to burn.'

This from a very ancient man whose father had been employed on the work. He had heard his father and mother talking about it once after they thought he was asleep. There had been more said. But that was all he could remember.

(I conjectured that the storm was that of 6-7 January, 1839, which seems to have been little less violent than its better-known forerunner of November 1703. It came from the north-west. Inter alia it did considerable damage to Bishop Longley's new palace at Ripon.)

The churchwardens' accounts were available and showed considerable expenditure on repairs to the church and work (nature not specified) in the churchyard in the February and March of that year.

'Well,' I said, 'that's about as much as we are ever likely to know. I doubt whether Mrs. Urch can do any more mischief, if she likes to give a repetition of her original performance now and again. I expect the tree, which would have been quite a small one in her time, was necessary somehow. There seem to be unaccountable but very rigid rules governing these things. Perhaps we shall understand them better some day.'

'You may be right,' said Phillipson. (I don't think I have mentioned his name before.)' Now I come to think of it, there hasn't been a direct male heir at any time since 1839 for her to try her hand on. All the same I wonder--'

I was not much surprised to hear a few months later that Mr. Phillipson thought the house too expensive and that he was conveying it to the National Trust and going to live elsewhere.

I believe that it is uninhabited now, so that if Mrs. Urch ever returns to it no one will be any the wiser or the worse.

I have also heard that the trustees would like to restore the sunken garden according to the plan found amongst Sir Robert's papers. But Mr. Phillipson is opposed to this, and while they think him rather unreasonable they feel bound to respect his wishes.

THE COXSWAIN OF THE LIFEBOAT

There is upon the coast of Suffolk a church which is locally believed to be haunted. The rector is a friend of mine, and as I do not want to expose him to the attentions of the Phantasmagorical Association or any similar body, I will not describe the place particularly. I will only say that the church is a large building in the Perpendicular style of architecture constructed of grey flint. The neighbourhood is popular with artists. If these details are sufficient to enable anyone to identify it he is entitled to any reward for his ingenuity which he can secure.

The ghost has never, so far as I know, had a name put to him and nobody knows anything of his antecedents. He has never actually been seen. But he may be heard very often. He dances and chuckles, not upon the whole malevolently, but is always careful to keep a pillar or some equally solid object between himself and his audience. He is very agile and no one has ever succeeded in cornering him. It is on record that once when the sexton was locking up he chased the ghost (who was being noisier than usual) from pillar to pillar all down the nave. Then up the tower staircase as far as the belfry. Still there was nothing to be seen. By this time the sexton was hot and out of breath, so he said rather crossly--'Hey, what are you a sniggerin' at?' A clear voice from amongst the bells replied 'It's not funny enough for two.' The rest, as Hamlet once remarked, is silence.

If the story of what befell me a good many years ago within sight of that church is not interesting enough for two, I must apologize. But I think it sufficiently out of the way to be worth putting on paper.

The church is not particularly rich in monuments. But near the font there is a mural tablet worth attention. It commemorates the crew of the lifeboat from 1850-69. During those years they underwent no change and rescued no less than four hundred and fifty-two shipwrecked mariners. That particular stretch of coast is still, I believe, regarded by seafarers as unusually dangerous. There is no anchorage within thirty miles and about four miles out there is a maze of sandbanks. A sailing ship which gets among them in bad weather is lost and even a steamship finds escape difficult. There has been talk of putting a light there more than once, but nothing has come of it. When there was more coastwise traffic (for the most part in small brigs) than there is now, the calls upon the lifeboat must have been incessant during the winter months.

After nineteen years of beneficent activity (I am quoting from the tablet) disaster came. On 31 October, 1869, the boat was lost with all hands. No bodies were recovered except that of Henry Rigg, the coxswain. I had often wondered what lay behind this. Had they gone on too long and allowed familiarity with danger to blind them to the fact that they had become too old for the work--as is said to be not unknown in the case of Swiss guides? Had the coxswain's nerve and judgment, upon which everything depended, failed at some critical moment? Although it was unlikely that anyone would ever be able to answer these queries, I put them to myself more than once. For some reason, which I could not explain, I felt sure that there was a story behind this catastrophe which removed it from the category of ordinary hazards of the sea, and I wished very much that I knew what it was. Irrational as I knew the desire to be, it refused to be dislodged. In fact it became stronger every time I saw the tablet.

One day when I was wandering, rather aimlessly I must admit, in the churchyard, I suddenly found myself opposite Henry Rigg's grave. I don't know why I had never thought of looking for it before. Perhaps I had assumed that in view of his station in life there would be no headstone, or at least a small and inconspicuous one which would be difficult to find. In fact, it was a large and massive slab of the pink granite which was popular for such purposes about the middle of the last century. Personally I have always thought it one of the ugliest monumental materials known to man, especially when it is polished so highly that it looks wet. There is a striking example in the memorial to the O.W.s who fell in the Crimean War outside Dean's Yard. In 1869 it must have been about the most expensive material which could be procured. The inscription was brief:

IN MEMORY OF
HENRY RIGG.

For nineteen years coxswain of the Life Boat
Who was drowned with all his crew off the
Anchor Shoal 31 October, 1869, aged 62 years.

When thou passest through the waters I will be with thee.

There was no suggestion that the stone had been erected by public subscription. Had it been, the names of the crew would have been recorded. I concluded that the Rigg family had paid for it, and wondered idly how they had managed to find the money. This led to some reflections on funeral expenditure in general. These might have been prolonged considerably and even have reached a pitch of moral elevation sufficient to justify their committal to paper, had I not had a sudden feeling that there was somebody close behind me. Of course the churchyard was a public place and anyone might have come up without my hearing his step upon the grass. It might be somebody who had some business with another grave; or an idler like myself who wondered what I was staring at so intently and had allowed his curiosity to get the better of his manners. Nothing could be more reasonable than either of these hypotheses. But all the same I was conscious of a feeling of discomfort; almost of alarm. I turned round quickly, but there was no one there. I think this disturbed me quite as much as any presence, however malevolent, could have done. I had felt so certain that there was someone. However, as there was nothing to be seen I walked away. When I had gone a little distance I glanced back. It was between three and four on a November afternoon, so the light was failing. But for a moment I could have sworn that there was an animal of some kind, either a black cat or a black dog, I couldn't see which, sitting on the grave. It was gone in a moment whatever it was. 'Some trick of shadow,' I said aloud, more to reassure myself than because I believed it, and walked on; perhaps a little more briskly. I did not look behind me again and was glad when I was out on the high-road and only a few hundred yards from my inn, *The Flood Tide*.

I had stayed there often before and was on good terms with the landlord. If business was slack I would sometimes ask him into my sitting-room after supper. He knew a good deal about the neighbourhood, and was seldom reluctant to impart his knowledge. In perpetuity he might have been a bore. But as an occasional visitor I found him very good company.

I told him that I had come upon Henry Rigg's grave in the churchyard that afternoon.

'Ah,' he said, 'that's a fine stone. Must have cost a deal of money to put that up.'

'Yes, so I thought. Did his family pay for it, or was there a public subscription?'

'No, Sir. It were not his family, for he hadn't none. Never married and kep' himself very much to himself, if you take my meaning. When he die a lawyer chap come over from Saxmundham and say he were executioner for the Will. And he have the stone put and choose the text. No, there were no talk of any subscription, for he were not liked. No, he were not. They couldn't hardly get bearers for the coffin, I believe, and there was some as said he didn't ought to be buried in the churchyard at all. But rector he didn't pay no heed to they. All he say were--Well, he'll be safer there than anywhere else I du suppose. And so it were done. But no, he were not liked, not even by his own crew, though he were a good seaman--to give the devil his doo--as the sayin' goes' (the last four words seemed to be added hurriedly as an obvious afterthought).

At this point a servant knocked at the door and said that the landlord was wanted in the bar. I have not mentioned that his name was Rust. He went off, not altogether unwillingly I thought, and about half an hour afterwards I went to bed. Sea air always makes me sleepy.

The next two or three days were unusually fine for the time of year and I spent them bicycling about the country. I was taking a belated holiday, having been kept in London all through the summer months by a book which I was writing: an occupation which necessitated frequent and lengthy visits to the library of the British Museum. The manuscript was now in the hands of the printer and I felt that a change of air and scene would equip me to deal with the proof. I took care not to go near the part of the churchyard where Henry Rigg's body reposed. This seemed to me to be a wise precaution, though I must confess that I felt rather ashamed of myself for adopting it. All the same I thought I should like to elicit some more information about him. So one evening I invited Mr. Rust to join me again. After a little miscellaneous conversation I came to the point. I think he was expecting me to do so.

'Well, Sir,' he said, 'I don't know as I can tell you much more. I were only a lad at the time.' (You could, but don't mean to, was my unspoken comment.) But by what I've 'eard he was a close-fisted old chap. And then his language. The fishermen aren't so particular as what you or me have to be with a position to keep up. But they du say that the way he went on at his boat's crew was like, well, like nothing--if you take my meaning. They wouldn't ha' stood it, but that he were a good seaman: and you don't find them under gooseberry bushes neither; no nor yet on apple-trees. And he live all alone, with one big black cat what were fierce enough to scrat your eyes out. And nobody knowed what he did to pass the time away, except that he were never seen in church. And then when he die and it come out that he had a mort o' money in the bank at Saxmundham--well, that made more talk. How'd he come by it and why didn't he spend it? That's what people wanted to know. But the lawyer wouldn't tell 'em and the bank wouldn't tell 'em, so they was as wise as they begun.'

'What happened to the money?' I asked.

'Why, he left it all to an old lady somewhere Acle way. But she hadn't hardly got it when the house where she lived all alone got on fire and she were burned dead to a cinder. So she didn't get no good by it neither. And as she were interstit, what they term, and 'adn't no relations, Queen Victoria took it. There was some as thought she did ought to be warned. But I never 'eard that it done 'er no 'arm. You'd ha' thought she had pretty nigh enough already, wouldn't you, Sir? But there, she had a long family to put out, and a widow-woman too.

'There were an auction of Rigg's bits of things. But nobody wouldn't bid for 'em, not a penny piece. So the lawyer chap he have them taken away in a cart. And the man what drove the cart slip somehow, and the wheel went over his leg, and broke that in two places. Went lame all his life, he did.

'Then nobody wouldn't take the house till the agent he got some strangers. And they didn't stop no more than a week. So then Lord S.--what own all this part--he say--Pull that down. And it were done. There's been nothing of it these many years 'cept a few mounds just outside the village. The old people say it's no place now; specially after dark. But that's as may be, for what I know.'

'Well,' I said, 'he must have been an odd character. Is there anyone left who could tell me any more about him?'

Mr. Rust looked at me for a moment without speaking. Then--'Odd, well, yes he were. And if I was you, Sir, I'd leave it be so. But there's old Dan Rix what were in the coastguard when that happen. He come up here now and again and if you was to stand him a pot of beer and a screw of tobacco he mought get talkin'. And then again he moughtn't.'

Luckily, Mr. Rix honoured *The Flood Tide* with a visit about noon on the following day. I was in as I had happened to have a number of letters to write. An introduction was effected without difficulty and I followed Mr. Rust's advice with good results. I will summarize the story I got in my own words.

Yes. He had known Henry Rigg for several years. Probably as well as anybody. Nobody knew him well. He did not like him. Nobody did. But as coxswain of the lifeboat there was no one to touch him. He (Rix) remembered the day of the disaster very well. He was wakened about dawn by the distress signals of a ship. One of the worst gales he ever remembered. Wind north-east by east; the most dangerous quarter. The lifeboat was launched as quickly as possible, Rigg swearing and cursing mote than usual. By the time the boat was away it was quite light, so he watched through his telescope. The ship was a small brig. Foreign certainly: perhaps Russian. She was on the Anchor Shoal and didn't look as if she could last an hour. He could see the men clinging to the rigging. There was a very nasty sea, but Rigg's steering was wonderful. The devil himself couldn't have bettered it. One funny thing he noticed. More than once he could have sworn that there was someone sitting beside the coxswain. Must have been the way the old boat-cloak he always wore was blown by the wind. All went well until the lifeboat was nearly up to the distressed ship. Then all of a sudden the helm was put right over. The boat broached and was gone in a moment. This was before the days of the modern self-righting boats. (I have omitted some maritime technicalities with which the story as told to me was embellished. It will be enough to say that the act amounted to murder and suicide. A shore-going equivalent would be for the driver of a car to turn it off the road at fifty miles an hour.)

The ship went to pieces a few minutes afterwards. There were no survivors, and nothing by which she could be identified ever came ashore.

'Curious,' I said, 'that Rigg himself, who seems to have been entirely responsible for the disaster, was the only one who--well, I can't say "escaped" exactly, but lived (if you can put it that way) to receive Christian burial.' Mr. Rix took a long draught of beer, and put down his empty mug.

'Ar: there's some as the sea can't drown, and others as it won't keep!' With which oracular utterance he stumped off.

After lunch the wind had risen considerably, so I thought that a walk would be pleasanter than a bicycle ride. I would go northwards along the top of the low sandy cliffs and return with the wind behind me along the beach. The tide would not, I knew, be high till six o'clock, so there would be a strip of firm sand available. I walked for a little over an hour, and it was past three o'clock when I turned down to the beach and set my face for home. There was every prospect of a stormy night, and the white water on the Anchor Shoal was very visible under a grey and lowering sky. Naturally my mind ran on the story I had heard. Local opinion evidently held that there was more in it than met the eye. But what more it seemed unlikely I should find out. It was solitary down there. On my right hand the cliffs were high enough to cut off any view inland. On my left lay the sea. Some three miles in front there was a small projection, you could hardly dignify it by calling it a headland, screening the village for which I was bound. Naturally I had the beach to myself. No one was likely to be about in the gathering dusk and rising storm. On the whole I was glad of that. The company, or even the sight, of another human being might be welcome. But on the other hand there might be people about whom I should not care to meet. Once I thought of turning up to the top of the cliffs again. But that would be rather silly, and the particular stretch which I was passing then did not look very accessible. I certainly wasn't going to turn back to where I had come down. So I held on.

Presently I saw a figure some little distance in front of me. He was standing at the very edge of the water. I was surprised that I hadn't noticed him before, and allowed myself to wonder for a moment whether he had just come up from the sea. But of course that was nonsense. He must have been sheltering, resting perhaps, on the lee side of one of the groynes which crossed the beach at intervals. I could not make out whether he was going in my direction or coming to meet me. After a time I saw that he was walking up and down; like a man keeping an appointment. An odd and uncomfortable rendezvous, I thought, and no one else in sight. I hope he isn't waiting for me.

I did not like his looks, so decided to strike up along the shingle until I had passed him, though it meant heavy going and climbing the groynes, instead of turning them at the seaward end.

When I got a little nearer I saw that he was dressed like a seaman of the last (by which I mean the eighteenth) century. In fact he reminded me of the illustrations in a copy of *Treasure Island* which I had had when I was a schoolboy. He wore a three-cornered hat, a boat-cloak wrapped round him and sea-boots. But for the fact that he had two legs he might have been Long John Silver himself. His hat was pulled down over his forehead and the collar of his cloak turned up: naturally enough as the wind had risen to nearly a gale and was very cold. I could see nothing of his face, for which I was thankful. There was something indescribably sinister, worse than sinister, downright evil about him. However, he took no notice of me. I looked back once or twice when I had passed him to make sure that he was not coming after me. The last I saw of him he was still pacing up and down.

When I got round the little headland there were, as usual, a number of fishing-boats drawn up near the bottom of the slipway which led from the beach to the village. As I made my way through them I received the impression that there was somebody dodging about among them. But as the light had now failed considerably I could not see him distinctly. In fact I could not be sure whether there was anyone there or not. But I thought so; though whenever I looked steadily at the point where I had seen him last there was nothing. Anyhow, whoever he was and whatever he was up to, it was no business of mine and I did not feel called to interfere. Pusillanimous perhaps. But if, as I more than half suspected, he had an appointment to keep in the direction from which I had come, interference on any pretext would not be likely to be very fruitful. I won't pretend that I was not more than ordinarily glad to find myself safely back at *The Flood Tide*.

After tea I settled down to read that grim, if entertaining, work of Anatole Le Braz--*La légende de la Mort en Basse Bretagne*--which was one of the few books I had brought with me. The inn-library consisted principally of Sunday School prizes acquired from time to time by various members of the house of Rust. From one standpoint the collection was very gratifying, but except for *Little Henry and his Bearer* (which I was delighted to meet again) it was not in the first rank as literature. For the moment at any rate I preferred the sombre stories of Anatole Le Braz. Now, the reader who gets as far as this may assert, when he has heard the rest of what I have to say, that I fell asleep. I cannot prove that I did not. I can only say that I repudiate the suggestion entirely. I *know* that I did not. Even if I did, my 'dreams' would not be easy to account for.

Quite suddenly I seemed to be looking through the pages of my book at a scene beyond. Every detail was very sharp, though the whole picture was on a small scale. It was exactly like what one used to see in the *camera obscura* when I was a child. Some ingenious arrangement of lenses, and mirrors too I suppose, threw a picture of what was passing outside on to a table in a darkened room. I suppose such a thing hardly exists now. It could not hope to compete with the films; though as a matter of fact I came upon one only about ten years ago in a queer old house in Edinburgh, not far from the Castle. The first thing I saw was a sandy beach. The light was beginning to fail and there were unmistakable signs of gathering storm. Plainly a reproduction of what I had looked upon not much more than an hour before. And here was the queer sinister-looking seaman whom I had passed. As before, I did not see him come. He was suddenly in the picture, walking up and down. I was intensely interested, as I felt sure that the other party to the appointment would make his appearance before long. I was right. After not more than a minute or two I saw someone coming from the direction of the village. He kept as close as possible to the bottom of the cliffs, which suggested that he was anxious to avoid being seen. That part of the beach consisted of loose shingle, and if there is worse going than loose shingle to be found anywhere in the world I should like to know where and what it is. (I will not dispute the abstract possibility: I merely repeat--I should like to know where and what it is.) He came on slowly, and presently the old seaman saw him and stood still near the seaward end of a groyne. When the newcomer reached the landward end he turned and ran down it with surprising speed, bending double. He would have been quite invisible from the far side, and not easy to pick out from the other, or from the top of the cliff. The general effect suggested an animal rather than a human being and was extraordinarily repulsive. He seemed to be dressed like a fisherman, but as he too had a boat-cloak wrapped about him I could make out no details. I could not see his face. He struck me as unusually short, almost a dwarf, and I thought he was slightly hump-backed. When the two men met they spoke a few words. (Which of course I could not hear.) Then something which looked like a small bag changed hands. The second man stowed it somewhere about his person and started to return as he had come. Then everything became dark and I could see no more.

I felt sure that there was more to come, so waited, looking down at the pages of my book. I did not have to wait long. The next picture was the living-room of a cottage; rather larger and better furnished than the average, but not particularly noteworthy in any way. In the middle of the room was a small round table above which hung an oil lamp. There was a good fire of wood and coal on the hearth and I noticed the little blue flames which old ship-timbers always give off. (Whether this is due to the salt which they have absorbed, or to the tar, or to both, or neither, I cannot say.) Between the table and the fire a man was sitting in an easy chair smoking a long clay pipe. Beside him on the table was a long tumbler nearly half empty from which an inviting steam went up. I had no doubt that this was the second man I had seen on the beach. Now that I could see him plainly I saw that I had been right in thinking that he was almost a dwarf and, if he were not actually hump-backed, very round-shouldered. He was swarthy, almost as if he had gipsy blood in him, and his face was not a pleasant one. It was mean and sly. At the same time, however, the jaw suggested courage and determination. I could not decide whether I should dislike him more as a friend or as an enemy.

His surroundings were comfortable enough, but it was soon obvious that he was ill at ease. From time to time he fidgeted in his chair and seemed to mutter something to himself. Once or twice he looked sharply over his shoulder. The only other occupant of the room was a large black cat which was pacing to and fro in regular quarter-deck fashion on the side of the room farthest from the fire. But for the light catching its eyes from time to time I should not have known that it was there. They glowed very green and very bright. It seemed fairly clear that the man was expecting a visitor--and not a welcome one either. This suspicion was confirmed when he got up, tried the fastenings of the shutters and satisfied himself that the door was locked and bolted. When he sat down he mixed himself another drink. Before he had finished it a very strange thing happened. I saw the key in the lock of the door turn and I saw the bolts slide back. I am as certain of that as I have ever been of anything. The door opened slowly and a man came in. Of course it was the first man I had seen on the beach--and I did not like him any the better at closer quarters. He did not take off his hat or turn down the collar of his boat-cloak. So I could make no more of his face than I had before. But I was quite sure that two more unpleasant characters can seldom have been found in the same room.

The little man was obviously horribly affected by the entrance of his visitor. But he stood up as if determined to put the best face upon it. (By this time I think he was at least half-drunk; or, as he might have put it himself, Three sheets in the wind.) The men did not shake hands and no word was spoken. The newcomer drew up a chair to the table and produced a pack of cards. The little man turned himself towards it and they began to play. The cat jumped up upon the table and sat watching with a baleful stare. I do not know what the game was and could not follow it very well. But it became clear that the ace of spades was the master-card, and the visitor held it every time. As hand succeeded hand the face of the little man became more and more ghastly until it was hardly human. If a cat can laugh I swear that that cat, which I was coming to dislike as much as either of the men, was laughing to itself. Suddenly the visitor stood up. He seemed to have grown larger and his head almost touched the ceiling. He was between me and the lamp, and his cloak seemed to fly out like the wings of a great bird, so that I could see nothing but blackness. I thought I understood what is meant by *darkness which may be felt* in the account of the ninth of the plagues of Egypt.

When the scene cleared there was a new picture. I was looking at a churchyard, which I had no difficulty in recognizing. There was an open grave and a man standing near it; presumably the sexton. One detail struck me as curious. There were several spades lying on the grass beside him as if a whole party of diggers had been at work. Then I saw the funeral procession, headed by the clergyman, approaching from the lych-gate. It came straight towards the grave. The corpse was not to be taken into the church. The coffin was carried by four bearers and there were no mourners following. As soon as the service was over each of the bearers took a spade and helped the sexton to fill the grave in. All five men worked with immense energy, as if there were not a moment to be lost. The clergyman (this also I thought unusual) stood by and watched them. As soon as the work was finished the party dispersed as rapidly as was consistent with decency. In fact they might almost be said to have run away. Once or twice while this was going on I thought I saw a figure of some kind just outside the lych-gate. But it was so indistinct, that I could make nothing of it. I could not even be sure whether there was anybody there at all.

When this picture disappeared I felt sure there was nothing more to come, and soon afterwards the maid came in to lay the table for supper. As this was my last evening I had Mr. Rust in later to help me pass it. We talked of general matters pleasantly enough and no mention of Henry Rigg was made. But I think we both felt the other was somehow *en garde*. Next morning I returned to London.

Well, there is my story. I could not make it more interesting except by some unwarrantable excursion into the realm of romance. I cannot pretend to say why my adventure (if you can call it that) befell me, nor to explain any of the details. But I think I can guess why Henry Rigg was not popular in his lifetime and why his memory was still odious in the pleasant little village of H---- more than thirty years after his death. And I have sometimes wondered whether the text which the lawyer from Saxmundham had placed on his tombstone had any secret and sinister significance.

THE PRIEST'S BRASS

The rubbing of monumental brasses in churches is one of the occupations which attract a large number of schoolboys, but are seldom pursued for long after reaching man's estate. The collecting of foreign postage-stamps is another. Some stamp-collectors continue and eventually amass very large and valuable collections. But I think they are exceptional. I never remember to have heard of a brass-rubber who kept on systematically for half a century or more. Yet a complete collection of rubbings of English monumental brasses would be of great interest and value. It would provide a record of costume, ecclesiastical, military, civil and female, such as does not, I think, exist at present, for a period extending from the middle of the thirteenth century until the beginning of the sixteenth.

After about the year 1500 brasses become fewer, but they are still to be found for another couple of centuries. One of the very latest must be that of William Broderip, Vicar-choral and organist of Wells Cathedral, who died in 1726. The matrix is all that remains now.

As stamp-collectors are known as Philatelists, for some reason which I think has never been explained adequately, brass-rubbers might fairly describe themselves as Chalcotribists--should they wish to do so.

Certainly Chalcotriby can be a pleasant enough occupation during the long days of summer. It meant sallying out with map and bicycle, if part of the journey had sometime to be done by train, and making one's way by little lanes to remote villages, where the appearance of a stranger is (or perhaps was--I am thinking of the golden days which were *regnante Victoria*) an event sufficiently unusual to cause some interest and even excitement. Whatever the present generation may have to say against the bicycle, I maintain that there was no better method of exploring a countryside in the days before the internal combustion engine had, in the emphatic phrase of Lord Grenfell, 'ruined the earth, defiled the sea and made the air dangerous.' Even now the bicyclist can make use of routes where cars cannot follow him, and probably sees more things worth seeing in a mile than the motorist does in ten. As everybody knows, the part of England in which the Chalcotribist will find most to repay him for his trouble is situated to the east of a line drawn from Hull to Bournemouth. Within this area there is no district in which a bicycle cannot be used.

My procedure was always pretty much the same. When I had found my village, which was sometimes not too easy, I began by calling at the Parsonage. Of course I had always written a few days beforehand, asking leave for what I wanted to do. (This was only refused once, in a letter which I thought very oddly worded. Soon afterwards I heard that the writer had created a considerable sensation by appearing in the pulpit with an umbrella in his hand. He opened this and held it above his head during the whole of his sermon. The day was fine and the roof of the church in good repair. A few weeks later he resigned the benefice, at the instance of the bishop of the diocese, and (I was told) announced his intention of devoting the remainder of his days to the cultivation of parti-coloured roses, and the drilling of ducks. I do not know what success he met with in either undertaking.)

If the incumbent was at home, I always found him friendly and usually hospitable; sometimes almost embarrassingly so. If he had to be out or away, I got a message to the effect that I should find the church open and that the sexton would be about to give me any help I wanted. If possible, I used to lunch off bread and cheese and beer at the inn, as that wasted least time while the light was good. If I was invited to tea I generally accepted, because by that time I had finished my work (if you can call it that) and was prepared to enjoy a little conversation about the place and its people before starting for home or for wherever I had arranged to pass the night. Not a very hazardous or very exciting way of spending a day, one would think. All the same I did once meet with what may fairly be called an adventure, which might have ended very unpleasantly. I have never understood it thoroughly and up to now only two people beside myself have heard the story. I do not think that any harm can come of putting it on paper after a lapse of more than forty years.

Much Rising will serve as the name of the village concerned, and I need not indicate its situation more particularly than that it is to be found within the boundaries of the old diocese of Lincoln, which anciently extended from the Humber to the Thames.

One fine morning in August, when the last century was nearing its close, I might have been observed (and in fact probably was) ringing the door-bell at the Rectory. The Rector made me very welcome. He said that my name was familiar and I soon discovered that he had been at Trinity Hall with two of my uncles, and intimate with one of them. Unfortunately both he and Mrs. Foster (I ought to have mentioned his name before) had to spend a considerable part of the day at the monthly meeting of the hospital committee in the market-town some miles away. As he spoke I heard the sound of a horse's feet and wheels on the gravel outside the window, as if a trap of some kind were being brought round to the front door.

'However,' he went on, 'you will find the church open and the sexton will be about all day as he has got a grave to dig. I've told him to expect you and give you any help you may want. We ought to be back about four o'clock, and shall be very glad if you will come in to tea before you start for home.' At this point, Mrs. Foster came in, equipped for the expedition. (Roads were often very dusty then.) I will not attempt any details of her costume, which would appear as remarkable now as the get-up of to-day would have done then. I was introduced, and the invitation to tea was repeated very cordially. Then--'Alfred, my dear, it's high time we were off. You know that if you are late, you'll find that they have made Lord Merton take the chair. And he always goes to sleep after the first ten minutes, and wakes up in a bad temper when we have nearly finished, and wants everything to be discussed all over again. I can't imagine why he doesn't resign; especially as when he is awake he never hears more than half of what is said.'

As I prepared to take my leave I said, 'By the way, what is the sexton's name? It might be convenient to know and I never like asking people directly, if I can help it.' 'Nicholas Clenchwarton,' replied the Rector. 'Odd, isn't it? And not the only odd thing about him either. However, we needn't go into that now. You can tell me what you think of him when we meet this afternoon. We really must be off now.' I thought that the last sentences were added rather hastily. Mrs. Foster's expression suggested that she had a good deal to say about Nicholas Clenchwarton's oddity and was quite prepared to say it, even if it meant finding Lord Merton in the chair at the hospital committee.

When I reached the churchyard, I found that the grave had made so much progress that the digger was invisible. The appearance of spadefuls of earth thrown up from below showed that he was there and hard at work. I advanced towards the place, but was still several yards from it when he climbed out, nimbly enough, and came to meet me. It flitted through my mind that it was a coincidence if he had decided to knock off work at that moment, and if he had heard my step on the grass his ears must be preternaturally sharp. Odd was certainly not an exaggerated description of him. He was very short, almost a dwarf and, as often happens with such people, very broad and deep in the chest. Obviously he was extremely powerful. His complexion was swarthy and his hair black. Both uncommon in that part of England. He looked as if he might have more than a dash of gipsy blood in him. Had his name been Mace, or Farr, or Lee, I should not have been surprised. He was not wearing a hat, and two tufts of black hair stood out above his ears, almost like horns.

There was something unusual about his face which I did not take in for a moment. Then I saw that his heavy black eyebrows met in the middle; as St. Paul's are said to have done in the *Acts of Paul and Thecla*. He looked as if he might have been a seaman in earlier life and I thought he would not have been out of place as one of the ship's company of the *Hispaniola*. Gunner's mate to 'that brandy-faced rascal Israel Hands' would have suited him very well*. [* See *Treasure Island*.]

We shook hands, and I mentioned that the day was fine. He assented, but added that the farmers would be glad of some rain. Then--'Be you the gentleman rector told me to look for?' and on receiving an answer in the affirmative, he jerked a thumb in the direction of the church porch, and said 'All ready.' As he seemed to be a man of few words, I left him, and he returned to his grave.

The church was small and, except for a fine Norman arch to the chancel, presented no noteworthy architectural features. There was little coloured glass (of which I was glad) and none of it old. The strips of coco-nut matting which covered the floor had been rolled up so that I could get at what I wanted without delay or difficulty. I decided that this should be worth half a crown to Clenchwarton.

There were five brasses to be seen. None of them of outstanding interest or merit, but worth a visit. The largest and most elaborate was of Thomas Ketton, Lord of the Manor, who died on 9 September, 1513. I wondered whether he had fallen at Flodden, but if he had, the fact was not recorded. At the foot were some lines which I think will bear reproduction.

Livest thou, Thomas? Yea, with God on high.
Art thou not dead? Yea, and here I lie.
I who on earth did live but for to die,
Dyed for to live with Christe eternally.

When I had finished my rubbings, I looked round to see whether there was another brass which I had overlooked. I could not see one, but I had a curious feeling that there was one somewhere. The impression became stronger, and I could almost have sworn that someone had whispered in my ear, 'Look again.' I turned round sharply. But of course there was no one. How could there be? I went out into the churchyard and told the sexton that I thought I had done all I meant to do and thanked him for his trouble. At this point my half-crown changed hands, and this may have had something to do with the fact that when I asked him to come to the church with me for a minute or two he raised no objection. When we were inside, I said to him, Now, are there any more brasses beside these five?'

He looked at me rather hard, and then with the air of a man who has made his mind up after a struggle said, 'Yew arsted me, remember that if things come orkard.' Having delivered himself of this enigmatic utterance he turned and stumped up the chancel. Just inside the altar rails he picked up the edge of the sanctuary carpet and disclosed a small brass, which I saw at once to be that of a priest, vested and holding a chalice. There did not seem to be anything unusual about it, except that it was in bad condition.

'Well, there he be. Du yew fare to take his picture?'

'Why, yes. Why not? I shan't do it any harm.'

Again he paused and looked at me hard. I began to wonder whether he were quite right in his head.

Then very slowly--'I du suppose not. But every seesaw has two ends, as the saying is.' With which he took himself off.

Closer inspection of the brass showed that it was very much worn. The face seemed to be almost entirely obliterated and the inscription round the edge was largely illegible. But as it appeared to be in its original matrix, I concluded that slab and brass must have been moved from some more exposed position: possibly with a view to the preservation of the figure. I knelt down and spread my paper and began to rub. But I must admit that as I did so I began to feel extraordinarily uncomfortable. It was as if I were setting in motion something which had better be left quiet and once started might be beyond control. Besides this, I kept fancying that someone was watching me from outside, through one of the windows, which were of clear glass. I seemed to get a glimpse of a face (and not a pleasant or friendly one either) out of the tail of my eye. But when I looked full at this window (not always the same one) there was nothing to be seen. Once I got up and went out quickly, but of course there was no one; only the sexton at work on the grave, which was too far away for him to have got to it in time.

I ran round to the other side of the church to make certain that there was no one there and then went back feeling thoroughly ashamed of my attack of nerves. I found that my paper had been moved to a distance of two or three feet and I had some little difficulty in replacing it exactly right. 'Draught from the open door,' I told myself. But I did not really think so.

Altogether I was heartily glad when I had finished and could make my way out into the sunshine of the afternoon. As I passed out of the churchyard I called to the sexton and said, 'I've finished now; you can lock the church as soon as you like.' His reply was indistinct, but I thought I caught something to the effect that there's those as locks and bars won't hold.

On reaching the Rectory, which was only about a couple of hundred yards away, I found Mr. Foster and his wife in a somewhat exhausted condition, especially the lady. The committee had been very long and *that* Mrs. Shorton (who appeared to be the Archdeacon's wife) even more tiresome than usual. However, tea and some extremely good cakes soon produced a more equable frame of mind.

'Well,' said the Rector, 'how did you get on? And what did you make of Clenchwarton?'

'Oh, I found all I wanted, thank you, and I think my rubbings have come out quite well. But I can't say that I took to him particularly.'

'Take to him!' exclaimed the lady, 'I should think not indeed. He gives me the creeps whenever I look at him. I'm sure he's a dreadful man. It would never surprise me to hear that he had committed at least one murder. I don't think he ought to be employed as sexton; and if I've said so once I've said so a hundred times.'

'Yes, my dear, I know you have,' rejoined her husband. 'But, as you know, I didn't appoint him. I found him here when we came, ten years ago, and have no reason for dismissing him. As you saw,' addressing me, 'he keeps the church and churchyard very well. He must have some money of his own (that kind of man often owns a few cottages somewhere), because he does no other work, and he could hardly manage on what we pay him. Of course in a small place like this the sexton's job is only a part-time one and is paid as such, because it is assumed that he has another. But Clenchwarton really makes it a whole-time one. He does more than he need, and more than we pay him for. I know he isn't liked in the village, but that may be merely because he is a "furriner" and keeps himself very much to himself. I have no idea where he belongs. If he has ever been married, he was a widower without children when he came here. But I don't know even as much as that. There is nothing to be got out of him about his antecedents.'

Mrs. Foster said nothing, but it was clear that she thought his reticence prudent.

'They say that he is out too much at night. But if he were a poacher he wouldn't be the only one in the parish, so I don't see why they should mind. But I don't think they mean that; in fact, I don't know what they do mean; and I'm not sure that they do. Anyhow the keepers have never caught him and I never heard of him getting drunk or anything of the kind. So I've nothing against him and he is an extremely useful servant.'

'There's one thing I should like to ask before I go,' I said. 'Why do you suppose he didn't want me to see the brass of the priest in the sanctuary?' and I told what had passed.

When he had heard my story the Rector said nothing for a minute or two. I thought he seemed to be rather disconcerted by it. Then he said, That's very curious. The man's name was William Codd, and when Bishop John Russell held a visitation in 1485 he was accused of practising unlawful arts. Of course the charges were vague and I don't know how seriously the Bishop took them. Bishops often showed plenty of common sense in such matters, more than magistrates. Codd died almost immediately afterwards, so no more was heard of them. There must have been some feeling against him in the parish though, because he wasn't buried in the chancel as the rector had a right to be. They put him at the west end under the tower.'

'I suppose it was then that the brass got so badly worn,' I said, interrupting, perhaps rather rudely.

Yes: I dare say. But anyhow the place didn't suit him and he seems to have made himself troublesome in a variety of ways. Eventually they took him up with the sanction of Bishop William Wickham (about 1590 that was) and put him where he is now. But stories live on in an extraordinary fashion in these villages, and I believe some of the people aren't so sure that he always is there; even to-day. I wonder how much Clenchwarton knows and what he thinks about it. But I don't suppose that you or I would get much out of him.'

Soon after this I took my leave. I had to bicycle about ten miles to the town where I had taken a room at the inn for a week. There were several churches in the neighbourhood which I wished to visit and the map had showed me that this would be the most convenient centre. I promised myself a pleasant ride in the cool of the late afternoon. There was no summer-time, then, and six o'clock really was six. But I was disappointed. As is usual in that part of England there was a fairly broad strip of grass on each side of the road. Then a wide and deep ditch, dry of course now, with a quick-set hedge beyond it.

As I rode along I could hear a rustling in the ditch, such as might be made by a small animal. Nothing out of the way in that, you will say. But what was out of the way was that the sound kept up with me, to be exact it kept about two yards behind, never more or never less. I put on speed, but even when I got some help from the ground I could not shake it off. Twice I dismounted and went to the ditch. But there was nothing to be seen. When I stopped, the rustle stopped. But as soon as I mounted it began again. I did not like it, but there did not seem to be anything to be done. When I got into the street of the town it ceased.

I had company at my supper and afterwards in the shape of a commercial traveller, who was not indisposed for conversation. Ordinarily I might have found this rather tiresome. But that night I must admit that I welcomed it. He gave me a most interesting discourse on the way in which different kinds of soap go in and out of fashion, and how the tastes of different villages vary and change. I gathered that to sell soap successfully in a country district you must have a considerable endowment of prophetic vision and be a close and sympathetic student of human nature. He obviously wanted to know what had brought me there. So I told him that I was having a holiday, and had spent most of the day at Much Rising.

'A queer place by all accounts,' was his comment, but as it was not on his ground, he had never been there. The town in which we were was the limit of his beat.

I went to bed early, but did not sleep very well. I woke up several times during the night, with an uncomfortable feeling that someone (or something) was moving about the room. Twice I struck a light, but no intruder was visible. The house was an old one and might well harbour rats. As long as they kept behind the wainscot they could do me no harm. With this reflection, which I did not find quite as comforting as the sterling common sense by which it was inspired ought to have made it, I went to sleep again.

The next morning was very wet. The landlord assured me that it would clear about twelve o'clock. So I thought I would occupy myself by going over the rubbings I had made yesterday. They had all come out well: Codd's surprisingly so. In fact I could make out more than I had seen when looking at the original. (This does sometimes happen, just as a photograph of a manuscript, especially of a palimpsest, may be easier to decipher than the manuscript itself.)

The lettering round the edge was very much broken, but I could read as follows:

... ISA AC ...... NDA MORTE PTVS DIE NOV .... INA CE VERE.

This I reconstructed--

IMPROVISA AC HORRENDA MORTE ABREPTUS XXIXno DIE NOVEMBRIS SATURNINA LUCE VERE.

He was snatched away by an unforeseen and dreadful death on 29 November, truly a day of ill-omen. (The year was completely obliterated. But the rector had told me that it was 1485.)

My restoration of the day of the month was conjectural. But I remembered that 29 November was the day of St. Saturninus of Toulouse, who was gored to death by a savage bull during the Decian persecution. And I thought that the coining of an adjective from his name, more or less equivalent to our *saturnime*, was not unlikely. I wondered what had happened to William Codd. Probably an accident, which, in view of the suspicions which seem to have been entertained with regard to him, was no doubt looked upon as a divine judgment.

The conventional prayer CVIS ANIME PPTIETVR DEVS (*on whose soul may God have mercy*) was not part of the original lettering of this brass. It was incised on the stone slab, rather roughly, and obviously by a later hand. This was out of the common and lent some colour to the idea that the parish discovered that it had not seen the last of him when his funeral was over.

'Well,' I said, half to myself and half to the rubbing on the table before me, 'I wonder what you really were like. Pity there's nothing of your face to be seen.'

And now comes the most remarkable part of my story. As I spoke some lines began to appear. At first they were very faint. Gradually they became definite, as a photographic negative takes shape in the developing dish. Little by little a face emerged, and it was a face I knew. I had seen it as lately as yesterday. There could be no mistake. There were the eyebrows meeting in the middle, and the horn-like tufts of hair over the ears. I was looking at a portrait of Nicholas Clenchwarton.

For some reason which I cannot quite explain I did not feel frightened. Partly perhaps because surprise left no room for any other emotion; partly perhaps on account of the prosaic nature of my surroundings. The parlour of an inn in a small country-town about eleven o'clock in the morning does not provide a convincing mise-en-scène for supernatural experiences.

While I watched, a further change took place. The face became less human; the tufts of hair were now definitely horns and I was looking at a bull's head on a human body.

'Like the Minotaur,' I said to myself. Certainly the eyes and forehead suggested more than bovine intelligence. In another minute it had faded away and the face was a blank again.

Had I been dreaming? No: I knew I had not. I saw what I have just described as plainly as ever I saw anything in my life. Obviously I must return to Much Rising as soon as might be and talk matters over with the Rector. As the landlord's forecast of the weather proved correct I put this plan into execution shortly after lunch.

I must admit that I began to feel a little nervous as I left the town. The road was a lonely one and I soon discovered that my companion of the day before was waiting for me in the ditch. However, I must go and I did not see how I could come to any harm. Presently, when I was in sight of the village, the rustle passed me, and about a hundred yards farther on I thought I saw a small animal of some kind leave the ditch and go through the hedge into a field. I only got a fleeting glimpse, and cannot say more of it than that it was of a darkish colour, and about the size of a rabbit. But a rabbit it was not. Nor was it an unusually large rat. A short distance farther on there was a gate into the field. As I came up to it, a man opened it and said, 'This is your way.' I saw that there was a large meadow with a well-trodden track, quite practicable for a bicycle, running across it. At the far side it disappeared into some bushes and just beyond them I could see the chimneys of the Rectory. It was part of the general oddness of the day that I felt no surprise at the fact that the man knew where I was going, any more than, I think, one is ever surprised in a dream. I thanked him, turned through the gate, and began to ride across the field. I only saw him for a moment, and afterwards could not recall him with any clearness. He had a broad-brimmed hat, so that I never really saw his face, and was wearing a long light-coloured garment; at the moment I took it for the smock-frock which was sometimes to be seen on old labourers then. On subsequent reflection, I doubt whether this theory was correct. That was as much as I could say, when I came to tell my story to the Rector, and he could not identify my description with that of anyone in the parish. Later, I seemed to remember that the man's voice had been curiously hoarse, as if from long disuse.

When I was about half-way across the field, I heard a noise behind me. I looked over my shoulder and saw a large black bull coming after me; obviously not with any friendly intention. Flight was my only chance, and the shrubbery or plantation, or whatever it might be, for which I was heading might aid my escape. I rode for all I was worth, but the path was narrow and rough, and I judged that the beast was gaining on me. As I entered the plantation, I saw what looked like a small disused quarry straight in front of me. There was only one chance, and that seemed a poor one. I wrenched my front wheel sideways and rolled over amongst the bushes. As I fell I heard a bellow and a crash. I picked myself up thankful to be still alive. The bull was nowhere to be seen. I presumed that he had gone into the quarry, and was well content to leave him there. I ran as best I could, staggeringly, blindly, through the bushes, and found myself at the gate leading into the Rectory garden. I opened it (thank goodness it was not locked) and ran on a few steps. Then I must have fainted, as the next thing I knew I was in a basket-chair on the lawn with a taste of brandy in my mouth and the Rector and Mrs. Foster beside me.

His first remark was very kind and wise. Don't try to tell us what has happened until you feel like it.'

But, like many people when they have been badly frightened, but not seriously hurt, I suddenly felt very angry.

'I call it disgraceful,' I said, 'to have a savage bull at large in that field. And that unfenced quarry, or whatever it is in the plantation, is an absolute death-trap.'

'Bull? Quarry? What are you talking about? All that land belongs to me, it's part of the glebe, always has been. The field is called Bull-Yard; I suspect that goes back to the days when it was part of a Rector's duty to provide a bull and a boar for the parish (did you know that, by the way?). But I don't suppose there has been a bull there for years. Certainly not since I've been here. And there's no quarry in the plantation. How should there be? There's a small depression where water collects in winter. It might be nearly up to your knees at times. But of course it's as dry as a bone now. You could have ridden your bicycle straight across it. I suppose there might have been more of it once. There are a number of small quarries in these parts, and some of them are still worked. But if that was one of them it was filled in, perhaps by nature, long ago.'

During this speech I became more reasonable. I apologized and said, 'Well, will you come and see?'

He would, and we went, and found it as he had said. The only part of my story which seemed to have a word of truth in it was that I had fallen off my bicycle into the bushes. At any rate the bicycle was there, not much the worse, I am glad to say, and my cap and some broken twigs. There was no pit or quarry and no trace of any bull.

'But didn't you hear him bellow?' I asked.

'I thought I heard some distant thunder. But it must have been several miles away,' was the reply.

Wild as my story must have sounded, the Rector did not upbraid me or laugh at me. He looked thoughtful and then said, 'I expect you'll have something more to tell me presently,' and led me back into the garden. We met Mrs. Foster coming from the house and she very kindly asked me to stay the night. 'You've had a shock of some sort,' she said, 'you really aren't fit to go. My husband can lend you all you want for the night, or you can have some of Gerald's things.' (Gerald, I learned afterwards, was a soldier son, who naturally left most of his belongings behind him when with his regiment.)

I made some feeble protest, but they both brushed it aside. 'In fact you must stop,' she went on. 'I have sent a telegram' (telephones hardly were in the country then) 'to the *Woolpack*--you told me yesterday you were there, and of course I know the people quite well--telling them not to expect you before lunch to-morrow.'

That settled it. I was really grateful to her, as I hardly felt up to bicycling back alone, even less with such company as I might have. At her suggestion I went and lay down on the bed in the room I was to have. I fell asleep and when I was roused about seven o'clock felt much better. After dinner I told the whole story, very much as I have set it out here.

As soon as I had finished, Mrs. Foster exclaimed triumphantly to her husband, There, what did I always tell you? You simply must get rid of that horrible man now.'

'You never told me that there was any connection between him and William Codd,' replied the Rector, not unreasonably, 'and if you had, I doubt whether I should have believed it. But even now, I don't see that I can dismiss him. What reason could I give? What could I say to him?'

'Say?--why need you say anything?'

And in fact, as you will hear, the necessity did not arise.

On one point we were agreed. The sooner my rubbing of the brass was destroyed, the better. So we went to the weed-heap in the kitchen-garden, deposited the paper there and applied a match. The flame ran round the edge of the figure in an odd way, and at one moment the blank face was surrounded by a ring of fire. However, it was all over soon, and a puff of wind dispersed the ashes. 'And that's that,' said the Rector as we walked back to the house.

I slept more soundly than I had done at the *Woolpack* the night before, though once or twice I thought the owls seemed to be unusually noisy.

We were finishing breakfast next morning, when the parlourmaid came in and said that the policeman had called and was wishful to see the Rector.

'Sorry to disturb you, Sir,' he said as soon as he had been shown in. 'But would you please come down the village? I think there's summat wrong to Clenchwarton's.'

As we went, he told us that no one could recall having seen him since dinner-time the day before. The woman who did for him had gone as usual in the morning, but had been unable to get in. No knocking or calling could elicit any response.

His cottage stood by itself, between the end of the village street and the churchyard. When we arrived, a few people had collected and were standing about. The Rector, who was a magistrate, directed that the door should be forced. This was done without much difficulty. The cottage was of the ordinary four-roomed type, living-room and kitchen on the ground floor and two bedrooms above. It was clean, but smelt curiously earthy. We found ourselves in the living-room. At the far corner a steep and narrow staircase gave access to the upper floor. Clenchwarton was lying at the bottom in an attitude which showed plainly enough that he was dead. In view of the narrowness of the staircase, it was thought better not to try to carry him up. The body was laid on an old sofa in the living-room and covered with a counterpane brought down from the bedroom. While this was being done, a certain amount of murmured conversation went on, and I caught 'Saved Jack Ketch a job, I reckon,' from one of the men. This appeared to be the general sense of the meeting.

When the doctor came, he certified that there was a clean fracture between the third and fourth cervical vertebrae. Death must have been instantaneous, and had taken place more than twelve hours previously. Clenchwarton had obviously been killed by falling down the stairs. Whether he had had any kind of fit which had caused him to fall could not be determined without a post-mortem, and as there was no suspicion of foul play it hardly seemed worth while to hold one.

I returned to the *Woolpack* that afternoon, and went home the next day. I did not feel inclined to rub any more brasses just then; especially in that neighbourhood. Afterwards other occupations and interests supervened, so my collection has remained as incomplete as many others.

The verdict of the coroner's jury was of course 'Death by Misadventure' and the body was interred in the churchyard on the south side of the church.

No relations could be discovered. He had owned some house-property somewhere in the west of England. But as he had made no will, and the solicitors who managed it for him and remitted his rents knew no more about him than anybody else, I suppose it passed to the Crown.

The Rector paid the funeral expenses out of his own pocket, and had the words REQUIESCAT IN PACE inscribed on the tombstone. Some people in the village were inclined to object when the meaning was explained to them, on the ground that the sentiment was popish. But the general opinion was in favour of them. As far as our knowledge extends, they seem to have been efficacious.

It is easy to frame a number of questions in connection with the episode. But I have never been able to arrive at a satisfactory answer to any of them.

THE END

Lightning Source UK Ltd.
Milton Keynes UK
UKHW040755300420
362566UK00002B/353

9 781849 027762